Second Chances

A Family's Love Story

Mary Lewis

PAGE PUBLISHING, INC.
New York, NY

First originally published by Page Publishing, Inc. 2018

ISBN 978-1-64214-248-8 (Paperback)
ISBN 978-1-64214-247-1 (Digital)

Printed in the United States of America

To the descendants of Emily and Marie,
my daughter and grandchildren:
Sarah, Christopher, Nicholas, and Makayla Marie

In loving memory of my mother and my grandmother:
Lucille Marie Lawton Weiss
Emily M. Bowers Lawton

Cover art by Ward Olson

The more you love,
The more you'll find
That life is good
And friends are kind . . .
For only what we give away,
Enriches us from day to day.

—Helen Steiner Rice

Contents

Part 1: Emily

Part 2: Marie and Traugott

Part 3: Marie and James

Epilogue: Emily

Family History

Preface

This book is subtitled *A Family's Love Story* because it tells of the love between members of one extended family: husbands and wives, parents and children, and brothers and sisters. It was generated by the stories my mother told me about her parents and grandparents and the cards, letters, memorabilia, and newspaper clippings that she saved throughout her life. This became the core of the book. Historical and genealogical information was incorporated in the story, but all else is fiction. Factual family details are provided at the end of the book.

My grandmother, Emily, was born in Denver, Colorado, in 1883, the daughter of Marie and James Bowers. Marie died when Emily was only four years old, and Emily and her two younger sisters went to live with the Davis family in Rockvale, Colorado. Emily's father, James, died when she was eight years old at which time Emily and her sisters were taken to Davenport, Iowa, to live with the Richter family. Part 1 tells about Emily's life in Davenport through a series of fictional letters to the Davises written by Emily from age eight to age nineteen. Part 2 goes back in time to tell the story of Marie's first marriage to Traugott Richter, again through a series of fictional letters by both Traugott and Marie. Part 3 is told through letters written by Marie to her second husband, James Bowers, and to her three daughters. A small portion of that part is based on two actual letters from Marie to James. The epilogue is also a fictional letter that tells something of Emily's life in later years. It is written by Emily as if it is a response to a real letter that she received from Maggie Davis Jones. These surviving letters are recorded in the "Family History" section. This final section of the book includes my own comments about the story, biographical information about members of the three families spanning three generations, information about the Richter homes and store in Davenport, and a factual family tree that shows those members of my family who lived during the time of this story (1865 to 1919).

Family Tree

Traugott Richter & Marie Schmidt
(1844–1904)   (1850–1887)
m. 1867

William	Carl	Louise	Nonnie	Marie	Henry
(1871–1938)	**(1874–1947)**	**(1875–1946)**	**(1877)**	**(1878)**	**(1880–1963)**
m. Blondina Martens	m. Jenny Kuhr	m. Henry Dunker			m. Minnie Stender
William (1897–1965)	Carl (1898–1952)	Marie (1896–1959)			Traugott (1904–1965)
Rudolph (1900–1977)	Catherine (1904–1991)	Henry (1903–1975)			
	James (1908–1973)				

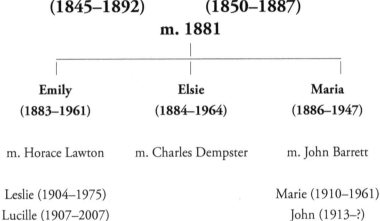

James Bowers & Marie Schmidt Richter
(1845–1892)   (1850–1887)
m. 1881

Emily	Elsie	Maria
(1883–1961)	**(1884–1964)**	**(1886–1947)**
m. Horace Lawton	m. Charles Dempster	m. John Barrett

Leslie (1904–1975)   Marie (1910–1961)
Lucille (1907–2007)   John (1913–?)
Mary (1908–1910)

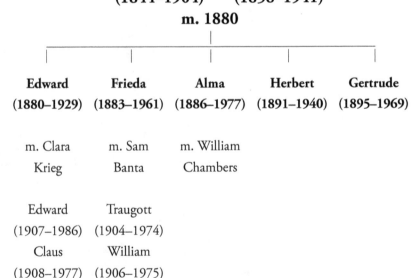

Traugott Richter & Wilhelmina
(1844–1904)   (1858–1941)
m. 1880

Edward	Frieda	Alma	Herbert	Gertrude
(1880–1929)	**(1883–1961)**	**(1886–1977)**	**(1891–1940)**	**(1895–1969)**
m. Clara Krieg	m. Sam Banta	m. William Chambers		

Edward   Traugott
(1907–1986)   (1904–1974)
Claus   William
(1908–1977)   (1906–1975)

Part 1

Emily

April 28, 1892

Dear Mama and Papa Davis,

We are staying in Pueblo tonight so we can catch the train to Denver first thing in the morning. Willie said that the train we will ride on tomorrow is very different than the train we rode from Rockvale to Florence and then to Pueblo because it has many cars that only carry passengers. It's not just one passenger car attached to a coal train. I just have a few minutes to write to you, but I will write a long letter when I get to my new home in Davenport. It was so sad saying goodbye to you. I already miss you so much. I am trying to be a very brave big sister just like you told me so Elsie and Maria won't be scared. Willie is taking good care of us. Before Papa died, he told me that I must trust Willie and go with him to Iowa. You said the same, but it still made me cry. Willie has been so kind to us since the day he arrived in Rockvale to visit Papa, and even though I just met him a couple weeks ago (at least for the first time I can remember), I feel safe with him. But I still can't believe that we are leaving you, and maybe I'll never see you again. Mama Davis, you are the only mother that I remember, and Papa Davis is my only father now that my own Papa has died. I know you are just as sad as I am, because I saw the tears in your eyes too when you kissed me goodbye. Please don't worry about us. I have to go now.

I love you so much,
Emily

*   *   *

May 1, 1892

Dear Mama and Papa Davis,

We are in Denver, waiting for the Burlington Northern—that's the train that will take us to Omaha. When we arrived here, Willie took us to the cemetery to put flowers on my Mama and Papa's graves. Papa's grave didn't even have a tombstone yet, but Willie said that it would be placed soon and would look just like Mama's. I asked when we could come back to see Papa's tombstone, but he said that might not be for a long time because Iowa is far away from here. We all held hands, and Willie said a prayer for Mama and Papa and asked God to watch over all of us and keep us safe. Will I ever come back to Colorado? Will I ever see both of you and Maggie and Ella again? It makes me want to cry when I think about that, so I can't think about it now. I'm still trying very hard to be brave for Elsie and Maria to set a good example for them. It's a lot of responsibility being the oldest sister. Willie let Elsie and me carry our dolls with us so we can hold them and sleep with them while we are traveling. We decided to change their names—Elsie said Dolly was a silly name anyway. Since I'm the oldest, I got first choice and I named my doll Maggie, and Elsie named her doll Ella. That way our dolls will always remind us of our two sisters in Colorado. I'll write again when we get to Davenport.

I love you,
Emily

*   *   *

May 2, 1892

Dear Mama and Papa Davis,

We are in Omaha now, waiting for the Overland Limited, the train that we will take to Davenport, so I have some time to write to you. There were lots of things to see and do on the train. The carriage where we sat was quite comfortable, and there was even a special dining car where we could go to eat— just like a real restaurant. There were white tablecloths and bouquets of flowers on every table, and the dishes were so pretty that it seemed a shame to eat food off them. But the food was really good. There was a lady and gentleman who looked very rich sitting across from us while we were having dinner. I heard her say, "I wonder why such a nice-looking young man is traveling with three little girls who look like street urchins." Then she asked her husband if she should report us to the authorities. I asked Willie if we were in trouble. He was not worried because he had papers to prove who he was and why he was taking us to Davenport. He said not to pay any attention to her foolish opinions because no one should judge people based on outward appearances. Willie said that we were sweet and good little girls and that's all that mattered. I'm glad that Willie is my big brother because he is so nice and kind and smart too.

The train went so fast it seemed like we were flying. It was hard to walk without stumbling when we went to the dining car. It was kind of scary when you crossed from one car to the next even though it's all inside. I liked looking out the window at first, but after a while, it all looked the same—not at all like Colorado with its beautiful mountains.

When I wasn't looking out the window of the train, I looked at my autograph album that Willie gave to me when he arrived in Rockvale. Everyone wrote a note to me before I left, and I like to read the notes again and again to remember my friends and teachers there. Willie also kept us busy by reading to us. He read a really good book called *The Adventures of Tom Sawyer*—Tom lived in a town just like Mark Twain's home in Hannibal, Missouri, on the Mississippi River. Willie told us that Davenport is on the Mississippi River too—I wonder if it's anything like Hannibal. Elsie and I would take turns telling stories and playing games with Maria. It all helped the time go by faster.

Willie also told us about Mr. and Mrs. Richter's family whom we will be living with when we get to Davenport. There are eight children, and there's even a nursemaid. Willie has two brothers (Carl and Henry) and one sister (Louise). My mother was their mother too, but Mr. Richter is their father. You see, my mother was married to Mr. Richter before she married my papa. The other four children belong to Mr. and Mrs. Richter. Willie said that he and his two brothers and sister all lived with us and my mama and papa in Denver before my mother died, but then they went to Davenport to live with their own father and his family. He and his brother Carl left Denver when I was only three years old so they could get an education in business and help their father in his store. Then Louise and Henry went to Davenport just a little bit later when our mother got too sick to care for everyone. He said I was just too little to remember them, but they remember us. It's just all very confusing to me. My mama wanted us to live with you after she died so our papa could still spend time with us. I was four years old, Elsie was three, and Maria was only one, so we don't remember our mama and that makes me sad, but I will never forget you, Mama Davis, because you have been just like a mother to the three of us.

I told Willie that we liked living with you, and I asked him why we couldn't stay in Rockvale with you. Willie said he knew I was very sad leaving all of you because you took care of us for over four years, but it was best now for us to live with our own brothers and sister because they are our real family. He explained that you are not related to us even though Papa Davis was our "legal guardian." I'm not sure what that means or why it matters because you seem like real family to me. I don't even know my real brothers and sister or all the other people we will be living with, except for Willie, and it's scary to be moving so far away to live with people I don't even know. I just hope they are all as nice as Willie. Willie said that his father, Mr. Richter, wants us to live with him, and he will be a good father to us.

I miss you, but I promise I will set a good example for Elsie and Maria and always be really polite and good for Mr. and Mrs. Richter. I love you and Maggie and Ella just as much as I could love any real family.

Emily

*   *   *

May 10, 1892

Dear Mama and Papa Davis and Ella and Maggie,

I miss all of you so much. I miss my school and my teacher and my best friend, Lottie. I miss my papa. I don't miss Johnny Jones because he always pulled my braids. We arrived in Davenport last week, and I've been so anxious to write and tell you all about it. Iowa is so different from Colorado. There are some hills and the trees are really big, but most of the country is farmland. Willie said that it is beautiful land because the rich soil provides food for people all over America. Willie told us when we went through Des Moines that our aunt, uncle, and cousins live on a farm nearby, and that's where my mama and papa met each other.

When we got to the train station in Davenport, Mr. Richter was there to meet us with a grand carriage that was pulled by two beautiful horses. He hugged us, and after he and Willie loaded our trunk, he took us to his house, which is very big and up on a hill that overlooks the city. But it's not like Rockvale where you can stand on a hill and see everything—the town, the valley, the hills, and the distant mountains. Here you only see parts of the city and the river because of all the big trees. I love the trees though because they are pretty. Davenport is a big city, almost as big as Denver, and much bigger than Rockvale. There were so many new people to meet that I can't begin to tell you everything in this one letter. All together there will be eleven children living in this house now, but Willie is really a grown-up and Carl is away in New York. I'm going to tell you about all of them in my next letter.

When the carriage came up to the house, a girl came running out to meet us. It was Louise, Willie's sister. She gave each of us a big hug when we got out of the carriage. She seemed so happy to see us, and she was happy to see Willie too. Willie told her that we were very tired from our long trip, and she could talk to us in the morning. Then we went into the parlor and were introduced to Mrs. Richter and Miss Anna, the nursemaid. We all shook hands, and Mrs. Richter invited us to come to the dining room for a glass of milk and piece of cake before bedtime. While we were eating, I overheard her telling Miss Anna that tomorrow, when the baby Herbie was napping, she was to wash all our clothes and throw out anything that wasn't salvageable. She said to look through the clothes that her girls had outgrown to see if there was anything decent we could wear. She said it was a good thing we were all little for our ages. I don't mind wearing hand-me-down clothes because it would be silly to throw out perfectly good things, but I don't want Miss Anna to throw away any of the things I brought with me from Colorado either. The next day I looked for Miss Anna and found her while she was taking our things out of the trunk. I told her that I didn't want my dresses thrown away because they were dresses that had once belonged to Maggie and Ella, my Colorado sisters. Miss Anna said that I was not to worry. She would wash them and iron them and fold them up in tissue paper and put them on the very top shelf in my wardrobe. She said I could keep them as long as I wanted—it would be our secret.

I don't think that Mrs. Richter likes us very much. She reminds me a little bit of the lady on the train. Maybe she thinks we aren't good because we are poor orphans. But I will be polite and try to make her like me. Mr. Richter is always very nice to us, and Louise and Henry and Edward and Frieda and Alma are very nice too.

Elsie and Maria and I have a bedroom just for us. Mr. Richter said that some time we might move into other rooms but he thought we would like to be together until we get used to our new home and family. Elsie and I share a big bed, and there's a little bed in the room for Maria, but she always climbs into bed with us at night. This used to be Frieda and Alma's room, but they had to move in with Louise for a while. I'm so glad that Elsie, Maria, and I get to sleep in the same room— even with all these people, I would feel so lonely without them.

I love you very much,
Emily

*   *   *

June 23, 1892

Dear Mama and Papa Davis,

The whole Richter family celebrated my birthday last week. They let me choose what I wanted to eat for dinner, so I asked for roast chicken. Then after dinner, they brought out a birthday cake with nine candles. I made a wish, but I can't tell what it was or it won't come true. Then I blew out all the candles. The cake was so good, and we had ice cream too. That was the best. Mr. and Mrs. Richter gave me a new doll for my birthday. She's a beautiful doll with eyes that open and close, but I don't like her any better than my Maggie doll. I named her Lottie after my best friend in Rockvale. I got some games and books from my brothers and sisters too. It was a wonderful day.

In my last letter I told you that I would write about my brothers and sisters. Of course, you know Willie—he's the oldest. Since Carl, Louise, and Henry lived with Mama and Papa in Denver for a while, perhaps you know them too, but that was five years ago. Willie went to business school so he could help Mr. Richter in the store. He told me that my mother used to help Mr. Richter with the store when they were married. Mr. Richter owns a fur store that is in downtown Davenport. Mr. Richter asked me to call him Papa Richter because all the other kids call him Papa. I think I can do that. Mrs. Richter wants to be called Mrs. Richter or Ma'am because she thinks that shows more respect. That's fine with me because she just doesn't seem like a mama. She never gives her children hugs and kisses like you did. I don't see her very much because she spends most of her time in the upstairs sitting room. Her life seems very boring to me.

Our second oldest brother is Carl. He's in New York City now, learning to be a furrier. I haven't met him yet, but he will be home from New York pretty soon.

Louise is seventeen, and she is really pretty. She has graduated from high school now and is working at the store. She helps take care of us and reads to us at bedtime and does just about everything else we need. She says that she helped take care of us when we were little, but we were just too young to remember her. She said that she missed us when she moved back to Davenport, and she's happy that we are all together again.

Henry is just three years older than me. He remembers us too because he was seven when he left Colorado and came to Davenport five years ago. He is always nice to us and even plays with Elsie and me some of the time. We go exploring together, but our favorite thing to do is going to the stable to pet the horses and give them apples or carrots. Henry, Louise, Carl, and Willie are called my half brothers and sister. It sounds funny to say I'm a half sister, but I'm glad they are so happy we are here.

The rest of the family are Mr. and Mrs. Richter's children. Edward is the same age as Henry, but he doesn't like to play with girls. Frieda is the same age as me, and she and Elsie and I play together. Alma is the same age as Maria, so they can be good playmates. I like all our new brothers and sisters, and they keep me from feeling lonely.

Herbert is just a baby. He's learning how to walk, but he doesn't talk yet—at least not words that anyone can understand. Miss Anna has a room up on the third floor, and she spends most of her time taking care of Herbie. He stays in the nursery most of the time. Miss Anna invites Elsie and me to come up to the nursery to play with him or sit in the rocker and hold him. Miss Anna is really nice, and she knows that we get lonely sometimes because all the others are still in school. Mr. Richter thought Elsie and I should start school in September because it's almost the end of the term now, and then Maria will be old enough to go to school too.

You can see there are lots of people living here. There's even a housemaid and a cook and a man who also works in the yard and takes care of the horses, but they don't live here. It's a good thing that this house is so big. My favorite place is the front porch that wraps all the way around two sides of the house. You can even see the Mississippi River from there.

One day I told Papa Richter that I didn't remember my mother, and I asked if he remembered her. He said that he loved my mother. I asked him why they didn't stay married. He said that he would tell me all about my mother when I am older.

When I start school, I will be going to Grammar School Number 3, and it is just a few blocks away from our house. Frieda showed us where it is, and we go there to play in the school yard sometimes. We just walk down the big hill to get there. Coming home is harder because we have to walk up that big hill. Sometimes I walk up backwards because it seems easier that way. I hope that I will be in the fourth class along with Frieda in the fall. She said that there are eight rooms in the school—one for each grade! It will seem strange not to be in the same classroom with Elsie. I can't wait to go to school, but I'm a little bit scared too. I miss you so much.

Emily

*   *   *

July 16, 1892

Dear Mama and Papa,

I just had to write to tell you what happened today because it made me feel so much better. When the day started out, I was feeling sad because I miss my papa and both of you and Maggie and Ella so much. I don't want to tell Elsie and Maria because that would make them sad too, and I can't tell any of the others because it would seem like I am ungrateful. So I went to the carriage house to talk to Ned and Nelly, the horses. I know that seems silly, but it makes me feel better. This morning I was telling them all about my papa and you and my life in Colorado and how much I missed everything, when I heard a noise above me. I called out "Who's there?" and Henry poked his head over the edge of the hay loft above me. I was so embarrassed that I started to cry, but Henry told me not to cry, and he would show me his secret hideout. He said to come up the ladder at the back of Nelly's stall. So I did. Then Henry told me that he understood just how I felt because he felt the same way when he had to leave our mama and papa and come to Davenport. (He was only seven then, the same age as Elsie.) Henry said that even though my papa was really his stepfather, he was still the only papa he knew then. He said that he wanted to cry all the time for the first few weeks he was here, but he had to share a room with Edward and he wouldn't cry in front of him. He said that Willie must have known that he needed to be alone some of the time, so he showed him the hay loft and said that it could be his secret hideaway. Now Henry said that he doesn't really need a secret place anymore, so it could be mine. Henry and Edward are best of friends now, and they like sharing a room. Henry said that it's all right to feel sad and lonely and it will be better in time. He said that Papa Richter will always be good to us and that any time I'm feeling sad, I could talk to him or Louise or Carl or Willie because they all understood what it was like to lose their mother and to move away from their home and live with people who were strangers. I feel a lot better already just knowing that someone understands my feelings. I know that you have been worried about me and Elsie and Maria too, so I wanted you to know that tonight I'm not feeling so sad. I still miss you terribly much, but I believe that we will all be happy again someday.

I will always love you,
Emily

*   *   *

December 3, 1892

Dear Mama and Papa,

I want to wish a merry Christmas to both of you and to Ella and Maggie too. It's hard to believe that Christmas is almost here and I've been away from you for six months now. I'm sorry that I haven't written in a couple of months. I get so excited on the days I come home from school and find a letter from you. I was happy to hear that Ella is getting married, but I'm sorry that she and Charles will be moving away to live on his ranch near Florence. That's not too far away, and there is a train that runs from Coal Creek to Florence, so you'll be able to visit. I think it would be so much fun to live on a ranch. I would want to ride the horses every day. Elsie, Maria, and I are all getting along fine here in Davenport. Papa Richter is very kind to us, but Louise is the one who takes care of us most of the time. She comes in each night to give us kisses, and then in the morning, she helps us get ready for school.

I remember last Christmas. It was such a happy time. Everyone in Rockvale gathered at the Town Hall, and there was a huge Christmas tree in the center of the room. I saw the most beautiful doll under the tree, and I closed my eyes and made a wish that it would be for me. Then when Mayor Baker picked it up and called Elsie's name, I had to try very hard not to cry. I wanted to be happy for my sister, but I was so disappointed that the beautiful doll was not mine. I knew that there were always many children who didn't receive any gifts except for the oranges and nuts that the teacher passed out, and I was so afraid that I wouldn't get a gift that year. Then I heard my name called, and there was another doll just like Elsie's, and it was for me! I think that was the best Christmas ever. My Maggie doll will always be my favorite because she reminds me of my home with you.

I'm in the fourth class at school. We had to take a lot of tests when we started school to see what class we belonged in. They said that I did really well in reading, spelling, and grammar, but that I was a little behind in arithmetic, so they put me in the fourth grade. Elsie is in the third-grade class, and Maria is in first. Our school is a brick building, and it seems really big to me. But there aren't nearly so many students in one class. My fourth-grade class has thirty students. In Rockvale there were fifty students in the school, and they were all in different grades but in one big room. Here there is a different room for each grade. First through fourth grades are on the first floor, and the upper grades are on the second floor. Henry and Edward are in the seventh-grade class.

I hope all of you have a very happy Christmas. I miss you still and love you.

Emily

*   *   *

August 12, 1893

Dear Mama and Papa Davis,

During our summer vacation, Elsie, Frieda, and I spent a lot of time exploring our town. Davenport has big brick buildings and streets just like Denver. It's a lot bigger than Rockvale. Papa Richter's fur store is in a two-story brick building on West Second Street. His store is really nice, but it smells like moth balls inside. His house is on Ninth Street, up on the bluff overlooking the river. It's about two miles away from the store. Sometimes Papa Richter lets us ride in the wagon when he, or Willie or Carl, is making deliveries or picking up supplies.

My favorite part of Davenport is the Mississippi River. It is a grand river that is one mile wide—I've never seen a river that is so wide. There are two bridges over the river here, so the trains and wagons can cross to Illinois. All the businesses and factories are near the river, and the biggest houses are on the bluffs overlooking the city. There are lots of beautiful churches, and many of them are built of stone or bricks. As you travel farther away from the river toward the farmland, the houses are just a normal size again and made of wood. The hills here aren't big like the mountains in Colorado. I miss looking at the snow-covered mountaintops like Pike's Peak and Castle Rock, but there are pretty sights here too.

One of the really fun things we did this summer was giving the Richter bear a bath. Papa Richter has a stuffed bear that he wheels out to the street in front of his store every day. Then at night he brings it back inside. Once every year in the summer on a hot, sunny day, all us kids go downtown to help with washing the bear. I think we got just as wet as the bear did. After we finished, Papa took us all for a treat at the ice cream parlor. That was my favorite part.

When we first started out exploring the city, Henry or Louise went with us. I think they were afraid that we three girls would get lost. After a few weeks, they let us go on our own—but not too far from home. Our favorite expedition is to go to the waterfront and watch the steamboats come in. There are always a lot of people, and the boats are really big. People say they look like floating wedding cakes. We have to be very careful when we cross the train tracks and not get too close to the river either. We love listening to the music of the calliope. Sometimes in the summer evenings, we can even hear it at our house. Some days we just go downtown to look in the windows of the big new store that's just a block away from Papa Richter's store. It's called Petersen's and Sons Department Store because they sell so many different things that it's divided into lots of departments. It's in a five-story red brick building that Papa said was designed like a very famous building in Chicago. I also like to go into Hansen's Hardware store just to watch the "mouse" run on a track. It's not really a mouse—it's like a little train that carries the money and sales receipts from the cash registers to the office on the second floor. Across the street from Papa's store is a German bookstore. Papa goes there to pick up the German newspaper, but I can't read German yet. Papa says that I will learn it in school.

My second favorite thing to do is read. I would be happy sitting on the front porch all summer long, reading books. Louise gave me lots of her books to read. My favorite was *Black Beauty*. After I read it, I went to the stable to tell Nelly and Ned how lucky they are to live in a nice stable and have kind people take care of them. Elsie and I play with our dolls, and Frieda has a lot of dolls too, but I don't think any of them are as pretty as our Maggie and Ella dolls. Some days we make a playhouse under the bushes in the yard, and some days we play in my secret hideout in the stable.

Sometimes I sit under one of the big elm trees and read stories to Alma and Maria. I like to read Hans Christian Anderson's fairy tales because Papa used to read them to Elsie and me. One day Mrs. Richter came out and said I should be teaching them something useful like sewing instead of filling their heads with fairy tales. When she turned to go back into the house, Maria stuck out her tongue. Afterwards I scolded Maria for behaving badly, but I really wanted to laugh at her instead.

I miss you and love you,
Emily

*　　*　　*

December 9, 1893

Dear Mama and Papa,

I can't believe that this will be my second Christmas in Davenport. Last year there was a beautiful Christmas tree in the parlor that was lit with candles. And can you believe—there were actually firemen that came on Christmas Eve to light all the candles? I am happy here, but I still miss you and Maggie and Ella. Please share my letters with Ella when you visit her. Elsie, Frieda, and I are the best of friends most of the time, but sometimes Frieda reminds us that we aren't really her sisters— we just get to live in her house. Louise said that she just says that because she is jealous that Elsie and I are so close and maybe a little resentful that she has to share her room with us. After we lived here for a couple months, Frieda moved back to our room and Maria moved into a room with Alma. Louise has her room back all to herself, but she says that when she gets married, Elsie and I can have her room. Louise has a beau, and I guess she must really like him since she talks about getting married. Carl and Willie share a room, but neither of them spend very much time here anymore. They are at the store from 7:00 in the morning until 6:00 at night. They usually eat dinner with us, but the younger children don't get to talk then.

I am doing well in school this year. I really like fifth grade. I especially like geography because we are studying the United States. When we studied Colorado, I got to tell the class all about living there and how beautiful it was to look at the mountains covered with snow even in the summertime. At school we read from McGuffey's Readers, but mostly I like to read at home when I can read good books. This year I read *Little Women*, and I put all of Louisa May Alcott's other books on my wish list for Christmas. I'm really good at spelling, so I try to help Frieda with her spelling homework. Sometimes she just can't remember the correct spelling, so I tell her to close her eyes and picture the word. When I do that, I always get it right, but sometimes Frieda still makes mistakes. Frieda is better at math than me, so she helps me with fractions and decimals.

Does the whole town still gather around the big tree in the town hall? It was always a happy time for me because I was one of the lucky children who received a present. When I got some candy, I would give it away to one of the girls who didn't get a gift. I always liked going to the schoolhouse for the singing of Christmas carols and watching the Christmas pageant too. I made a Christmas card for you at school—we learned how to do cut paper designs, so I decorated the card with snowflakes. I hope you like it. Merry Christmas to all of you. I miss you.

Love,
Emily

*   *   *

August 21, 1894

Dear Mama and Papa,

I'm anxious to go back to school in September and start sixth grade. Elsie will be in fifth grade and Marie in third. I love school and I miss it during the summer vacation, but we have a lot of fun during the summer too.

My job at home is taking care of Herbie—he's three years old now. Miss Anna is still the nursemaid, but she also helps with the cooking and cleaning. Frieda and Elsie are in charge of Alma and Maria, but since they are eight, they don't need to be watched all the time, and they can all do girl things together. I must really keep a constant eye on Herbie—he's always finding something to get into that he's not supposed to do. Then he screams when I tell him to stop, and I get in trouble if he does something bad. I'm learning how to get him to mind me better. When he starts doing something he shouldn't do, I distract him with another toy or game rather than just telling him no.

Sometimes he throws a temper tantrum at dinnertime and gets taken to his room, but usually when I play with him, he is good. He loves to laugh, and he's very smart too. I've already taught him the alphabet and how to count to twenty. At night, I read a book to him before he goes to sleep. I think he really likes that because he wants me to read it over and over again.

Papa and Mrs. Richter took us to a picnic at the Iowa Soldiers' Orphans' Home last week. The younger children had to stay home with Miss Anna, and Louise, Carl, and Willie went with their friends. Henry, Edward, Frieda, Elsie, and I all got to ride in the buggy. The orphans' home was way on the other side of the city, almost out in the country. Papa said that it was built for orphans of the Civil War soldiers, but now it is for orphans from all over Iowa or any child whose parents are unable to care for them. It seemed like the whole town was there for the picnic. There was lots of food and games, and a band played patriotic songs. It made me sad to see how many children don't have mothers or fathers or anyone else who loves them. They live in little cottages with lots of other boys or girls and a matron to take care of them. They all were having fun at the picnic, and everyone played together. The boys had a tug-of-war and a baseball game. The girls played jump rope. Everyone played hide-and-seek together. Henry's friend, Horace, found my hiding place. I'm glad Horace is the one who found me—he's really cute and nice too.

When we were getting our food, Mrs. Richter said to me that I would have had to live someplace like this if it hadn't been for her and Papa Richter taking us three girls into their home. That really scared me. I can't imagine living in an orphanage, but I told her that I would go back to Colorado to live with you. Then I just walked away because I didn't want to start crying in front of her. If we couldn't live with the Richters, could we come back to live with you? We are old enough now that we could be a big help to you, and I could even get a job to help with expenses. I don't ever want to live in an orphanage.

I didn't feel like eating or playing after that, so I just sat under a big oak tree and watched the others. When Papa Richter saw me all alone, he came over and sat down by me and asked what was wrong. I told him that I was scared that I might have to live in an orphanage someday and that made me sad. He put his arm around me and said that I never should worry about that. He said I can always live with him because he loves me and Elsie and Marie just as much as he loves all his own children. Then he hugged me and said that I was his "special pride and joy." I don't know why he feels that I'm his special pride and joy, but I'm sure glad that he does. I'll always try to make him proud of me.

Papa Richter told me how sad he was when my mother died and then how he worried about us when my papa died. He said bringing my sisters and me to live in Davenport with his family was a blessing for him. He called us his second chance. I don't know what he meant by that either, but even though he was smiling at me, he had tears in his eyes. I really do believe Papa Richter when he says that he loves us, but I know there is still something that makes him sad. I hope that I can help make him happy too because I like him so much, and I like living with all my brothers and sisters too.

I miss you very much,
Emily

*   *   *

December 9, 1894

Dear Mama and Papa,

Thank you for the letter you wrote to me in the fall. It makes me feel good to know that you would want us to come back and live with you if we could. I'm not scared any more, and I am happy here with so many brothers and sisters and Papa Richter. Most of the time, Mrs. Richter is nice too. I don't want you to think that she is mean to us—it's just that sometimes she says things that hurt my feelings. I don't think she was happy about taking three extra little girls into her home. Just like at first Frieda didn't want to give up her room, but now Frieda likes us and we like her a lot. Maybe someday Mrs. Richter will like us a lot too.

Louise got married this fall. The wedding was at our house, so we all got to watch the ceremony. Her husband's name is Henry (so we have another Henry in the family now). Henry lived in the house just across the street from us, so Louise has known him for a long time. He is an attorney in downtown Davenport, so they often walked home together after work. I'm not sure when they fell in love, but I know he would stop by the store and take her out for lunch. In the summertime, Louise would pack a picnic lunch for them and they would take it to the riverside to eat together. Sometimes he would come to the house to visit Louise. Elsie, Frieda, and I would try to spy on them to see if he would kiss her. But they always caught us, and then we would get sent to our room. I really miss Louise now that she has moved out of the house because she was the one I could always talk to when I needed someone to listen or give me advice. She also did a lot of the baking, so everyone will miss her pies and cakes too. She wants Elsie and me to move into her room now—I hope we get to do that because it will make us feel like she's still with us.

We've just had a big snowstorm in Davenport, and it's so beautiful to see all the trees covered in snow. When the sun shines on the snow, the whole world seems to sparkle. Every winter all the girls build a big snowman in the front yard, and everyone goes ice skating together. The boys love to go bobsledding down the hills. They use the huge sled from the coal company to sled down Gaines Street. They usually start at the top of the hill on Eighth Street and sled all the way to the bottom on Fifth Street or even farther. Twenty boys can sit on one sled. Some days Frieda, Elsie, and I stand near the bottom of the hill to watch. It looks like they are having so much fun. Sometimes the sled turns over before they get to the bottom, and they all go flying off and get buried in the snowdrifts. Once a policeman saw them and told them they had to stop because it was dangerous to go sledding in the street and flying across so many intersections. A horse and carriage could come along, and everyone's life would be in danger. After that, the boys started asking us girls to "guard" the intersections. We stand by and make sure that no one is coming down the street and then raise our arms to signal when it is safe.

I hope that all of you have a merry Christmas. It will be a special Christmas for Maggie since she can celebrate it with her new beau. Wesley sounds nice, and I'm also glad that he is from Rockvale so Maggie won't be moving away when she gets married. Tell Maggie that I am happy for her.

Merry Christmas with love,
Emily

* * *

July 28, 1895

Dear Mama and Papa Davis,

There have been some big changes in the family this year. Mrs. Richter gave birth to a little baby girl just a couple of days before my twelfth birthday. Her name is Gertrude, but everyone calls her Trudy. She is a cute, pudgy-faced little baby with a good disposition. Miss Anna devotes most of her time to Trudy now, so I'm in charge of Herbie more often than before. He's easier to handle now that he is four and can understand more. He doesn't have temper tantrums anymore, and he always behaves for me, but he can be mischievous too. When he does something that he's not supposed to do, he just looks at you with a grin on his face, waiting to see what you will do. Sometimes I get a break from babysitting, and Elsie or Frieda take over. Now that Maria and Alma are nine, they can do a lot of things on their own. But if they want to go play at the school yard, one of us older girls must go with them. Sometimes we all walk downtown to look in the stores, and we still like to go to the riverfront to see the paddlewheel steamers. Just think, Maria is the same age that I was when I came here to live—that was three years ago now.

Will has moved out of the house because he was married in the spring. (Now that he is a grown man, he doesn't want to be called Willie any longer, but sometimes I still forget to say Will instead of Willie.) Blonnie and Will were married at Grace Episcopal Cathedral. It was such a beautiful wedding in the elegant church with its stained-glass windows and high vaulted ceiling. Everyone was invited to Blonnie's home after the ceremony for cake and tea. Mrs. Richter thought that it wasn't appropriate to include the children, but Will told her that it would spoil his day if all his sisters weren't there. Of course, Herbie and baby Trudy stayed home, and then at the last minute, Mrs. Richter couldn't attend either because she was not feeling well. I'm so glad that Will insisted we could come, and Blonnie said that we all behaved like perfect little ladies.

I have to tell you about my big adventure this summer. But it's supposed to be a secret, so please don't let anyone know—I'm only telling the two of you. One day Henry asked Elsie and me if we would like to go on an exploring expedition to someplace we've never been. He said that we would have to keep our expedition a secret. We couldn't tell anyone else in the family, not even Frieda or Edward or Alma or Maria. That sounded mysterious and exciting, so of course we promised never to tell—but that doesn't mean you. Then Henry told us that he was going to show us the house where our mama lived when she was married to Papa Richter. We went down Ninth Street hill to Marquette Street and then a couple blocks up the street until we came to a big wrought iron gate with brick gate posts. The name Petersen's Knoll was engraved on a plaque on the gate. Henry said that we couldn't go in the gate or up the road because we would be trespassing. We had to sneak around through the yard and keep hidden behind the trees. If we saw anyone, we were to duck under a bush. There were lots of trees and bushes, so that part seemed pretty easy. When we got to the top of the hill, we saw the house for the first time. It was even bigger and more beautiful than the house we live in now. It looked like a castle, and Henry said that when Papa Richter lived there with our mother, the house was named Marie's Castle. Henry never lived there because he was born in Des Moines after our mother left Davenport. I wanted to walk all around the house to see it from every side, but we saw a carriage coming up the driveway, so we had to run away. I don't think anyone saw us.

When we got home, I asked Henry lots of questions about my mother and Papa Richter and why she left. He said that they got divorced. I didn't know what that meant so he explained that it's like getting unmarried. He told me I was too young to understand all of it. That's what everyone says when I ask about my mother, so I'm going to write down my questions in my journal so that someone can answer them for me when I'm old enough to understand. This is what I want to know:

1. Why did my mother leave that beautiful house? If I lived in a castle, I would feel just like a princess, and I would never leave it.

2. Why did my mother and Papa Richter get divorced? He is always so nice, and he even told me once that he loved my mother. Everyone tells me that my mother was beautiful and smart, so why didn't they just stay married to each other? I thought that when you fell in love and got married, you lived happily ever after, just like in the stories. Of course, I'm glad that my mother married my papa, because if she didn't, I wouldn't have been born. My papa used to tell me how much he loved my mother and how much she loved me. And I love my papa and Papa Richter too, so I guess we can all love many different people. I sure don't understand much about marriage.

3. Why did Papa Richter marry Mrs. Richter? She is very pretty, but she never smiles. Why is she unhappy? One time Henry told me that she's unhappy because her life didn't turn out the way she expected. It seems like she has a good life, so that doesn't make sense to me. I think that if she spent more of her time doing things with her children, she would be a lot happier.

If you know any of the answers to my questions, I'd sure like to hear them now instead of "when I am older."

I love you,
Emily

*   *   *

December 7, 1895

Dear Mama and Papa Davis,

I didn't really expect you to be able to answer my questions. I know that you and my papa were good friends, and you didn't know my mother when she was married to Papa Richter. I just wish I could remember my mother. I don't even have a photograph of her. But everyone tells me nice things about her, and both my papa and Papa Richter told me how much she loved us.

I'm glad that I can still remember my own papa. I certainly remember how excited I would be when he was coming to Rockvale for a visit. I remember sitting on his knee and telling him all about school and taking walks with him around town. We would walk down Main Street and visit Eaton's General Store. Papa would buy a licorice stick for each of us. Sometimes we would walk out into the country and climb to the top of one of the hills. Papa would tell us the names of all the mountains that we could see in the distance. Sometimes he would walk along the train tracks with Elsie and me and help us pick up the pieces of coal that dropped from the trains. He always made our job seem like a game instead of a chore. He read a story to us every night at bedtime. My favorite story was "The Ugly Duckling," because when I said that I hoped I would grow up to be like the beautiful swan, Papa said that he knew I would because I looked just like my beautiful mother. That always made me so happy. Sometimes he would read one of Shakespeare's sonnets. He said they would give us good dreams because our mother used to love reading Shakespeare. Whenever he was leaving to go back to Denver, he always said, "I love you, and your mother loved you."

I remember when Papa came to live with us again in Rockvale just before he died. I knew he was very sick because he couldn't get out of bed most of the time, but he always wanted us girls to visit his bedside and talk to him. As soon as I got home from school, I would go to see him and tell him what I learned in school that day. Sometimes he would fall asleep while I was talking to him. Then he would rouse himself again and look at me with a smile on his face and whisper, "I love you." Elsie and I have his photograph on the night table in our room.

I'm having a great year in school. There is so much to learn in seventh grade. My favorite subject this year is history. I love learning all about the settlers coming to America, like my own mama and papa did. We learned all about the beginnings of our country and all the presidents. My favorite is Abraham Lincoln. I love reading the stories about him growing up on the frontier—but back then the frontier was in Illinois, east of the Mississippi. I think that living with you in Rockvale was a lot like growing up on the frontier. I admire Lincoln for being self-educated, honest, and of course, for ending slavery. We memorized the Gettysburg Address in school. We are a nation "dedicated to the proposition that all men are created equal," just as President Lincoln stated. Our teacher, Miss Stricker, says that the belief in individual freedom for all people is part of our German heritage too, and that's why Germans were so opposed to slavery. Did you know that when Abraham Lincoln was a lawyer in Springfield, he defended the railroad's right to build a bridge across the Mississippi? That was the very first bridge across the Mississippi River, and it was right here in Davenport. I like knowing that I have those connections to such a great man. In school we also have singing lessons from Professor Otto once a week and gymnastic classes with Herr Reuter. When the weather is nice, we do our exercises out in the school yard. I love school, and I hope that I can grow up to be a teacher someday.

Elsie, Maria, and I wish you a very Merry Christmas. Please give our greetings to Ella and Maggie and their husbands too.

With my love,
Emily

*　　*　　*

December 5, 1896

Dear Mama and Papa Davis,

I was so excited when I heard that Maggie has a little baby girl, and now you have a grandbaby living nearby. I'm glad that Maggie and Wesley named her Maude after you. Papa, maybe Maggie's next baby will be a boy and she can name him John after you. I hope that someday I can come back and visit you, Maggie, Ella, and their families and meet baby Maude and Ella's two boys. Louise had a baby girl this year too. She named her Marie. When I asked her why she named her Marie, she told me that she hoped her baby would grow up to be a courageous and independent woman, just like our mother, Marie. So I tried asking Louise why our mother and Papa Richter got a divorce, but she said that same thing everyone says that she would tell me about it when I get older. I'm thirteen years old and in eighth grade—when will I be old enough?

I told Louise that I was really excited about being a "half aunt." Louise said that I should never call myself that—I'm baby Marie's aunt and her sister. She said that it doesn't matter that we had different fathers; it's what is in your heart that matters, and in our hearts, we are true sisters. She said that Will, Carl, and Henry all think of Elsie, Maria, and me as their very own true sisters.

Carl married Jenny Kuhr this past fall on a lovely day. I love autumn when the trees are covered in gold, orange, and red leaves. It was a beautiful ceremony at the Presbyterian Church followed by the most elegant reception at the Outing Club. The house seems a bit lonelier now that Willie, Carl, and Louise have all moved away. Herbie got to move out of the nursery, so he's happy that he doesn't have to share a room with baby Trudy anymore.

This summer I got a bicycle for my thirteenth birthday. I practiced riding on the sidewalk before I took it out on the street. Everyone says that the new safety bicycles are much easier to ride than the old ones that were so much higher off the ground with their big front wheel. Papa said that I had to stay close to home and never ride down the steep hills. Maybe next year he'll let me ride farther away from home but never down the Ninth or Vine Street hills. I wish I could ride my bike out to Duck Creek. That's where all the boys go to play and swim in the creek, but we girls aren't allowed to go there. Henry says that it's so much fun to jump off the tree branches into the big pools of cool water. I can't swim, but I'd just like to take off my shoes and wade in the water and explore the creek and ravines and woods.

Frieda has a bike too, so sometimes we ride over to the pasture on Tenth Street and watch Henry, Ed, and their friends play baseball. They choose up sides before each game. Frieda and I always cheer for them, but they usually ignore us. Secretly I cheer for their friend, Horace, because he has always been so nice to me. I don't think any of them pay much attention to us because we seem like little girls now that they are in high school. Henry and Ed go to Davenport High School, and Horace goes to Ambrose Academy because his family is Catholic.

Just before school let out for the summer, the principal, Mrs. Melville, called me into her office. I couldn't imagine what that was about—I've never been called to the principal's office before. When I got there, she shook my hand and congratulated me for being the school winner of the Kuhnen Medal. I was so happy. The Kuhnen Medal is awarded to the most outstanding student in the school that year. The teachers and principals make the selection. Everyone said it was very unusual for a seventh grader to win. Henry won it one year too, so I'm proud to follow in his footsteps.

Merry Christmas and happy New Year!

I love you,
Emily

*   *   *

December 11, 1897

Dear Mama and Papa Davis,

It's hard to believe that it's my last year of grammar school. I've been living in Davenport and going to school here for six years now. It's been a good six years for Elsie, Maria, and me, and we have come to truly feel like this is home for us now. You know how frightened I was when I left you. There were times when I didn't think I could ever be happy again. Now it is sometimes hard for me to remember Colorado, but of course, I will always remember you. Your letters keep my childhood memories alive too. Does my playmate, Lottie, still live in Rockvale? I guess I was just too young when I moved away to keep up correspondence with my girlfriends there. But your loving letters helped me through all the hard times. It's a good thing that I could write my feelings to you or I might have made everyone here angry with me. Now, I keep a journal so I can write about my feelings, and that always helps. I keep it in the locked drawer of my desk where I keep my other treasures. The key to that drawer is around my neck all the time because I don't want anyone to ever read my journals. They would think me very ungrateful. The letters from you are in that drawer, along with all the cards and notes that I get from Maggie or Ella. The autograph book that Will gave me when we left Colorado is there too. In time, I'll probably put the Kuhnen Medal away in the drawer too, but for now I keep it out on a little pin cushion that Papa gave me just for the medal. Seeing it reminds me to always work hard in school and to do my best.

Herbie started school this year. He's in first grade, and I imagine that he's the smartest child in the room. I've already taught him how to read and write and do some sums too. Elsie, Alma, Marie, and I always walk him to and from school.

Will and Blonnie had a baby boy this year. They named him William. Elsie and I rode our bikes to their house so we could visit. Now I have both a niece and a nephew.

I've been reading in the *Davenport Times* about the miner strikes that have been going on for almost two years in Leadville. I hope that you haven't had problems in Rockvale. I know that the miners deserve to have safe working conditions, but sometimes the strikes turn violent and then no one is safe. I worry about all of you and what would happen to Papa's saloon if no one had any money to spend. Please write soon and let me know that you are all okay.

Wishing you a Merry Christmas and Happy New Year.

Love,
Emily

*   *   *

July 21, 1898

Dear Mama and Papa Davis,

I just had to write to you to tell you about Henry. He has enlisted in the National Guard and is now off to fight in the war with Spain. I am so worried, and I pray every night that God will keep him safe.

Last February after the sinking of the battleship *Maine*, Henry started talking about enlisting in the National Guard. He and Papa Richter had some heated discussions about it for many nights after dinner. Henry thought that it was America's responsibility to help the Cubans with their struggle for independence. He said that he was sickened by the stories he read about the atrocities committed against the Cuban people by the Spanish. Papa said that the newspapers were misleading us with their sensationalism and overblown presentations of propaganda instead of facts. Papa agreed with President McKinley and many other Republicans that America should stay out of the war. I didn't know who was right. I understood Papa's point of view, and I certainly didn't want Henry to go to war. He always seems to be aware of the needs of others and will do whatever he can to make things better, whether it's for family, friend, or stranger. He doesn't want to go to war because he likes fighting; he just wants to help anyone who is being treated unfairly. Papa said that Henry would give away his last dime. Henry doesn't have any idea how terrible war is, and Papa hoped that Henry wouldn't have to suffer to have his eyes opened.

In March, America declared war against Spain. I guess the public opinion demanding war overwhelmed President McKinley's desire to avoid it, and Henry, like thousands of other young men, wanted to sign up immediately. Finally, Papa told him that he would give him his blessing if he would just wait until he graduated from high school in June. I know Henry hated arguing with Papa, so he agreed to the compromise. Then just two days after graduation, Henry had signed up for the National Guard and was sent off to train for the cavalry. Henry always loved horses and he's a good rider, so I know he was anxious to serve in the cavalry. We received a letter from Henry saying that he was being sent to Puerto Rico. So please keep Henry in your prayers too so God will know what a kind-hearted person he is, and I know He will watch over him.

The most important event for me this year was my graduation. Since I had won the Kuhnen Medal when I was in seventh grade, I was one of the speakers at the ceremony. I was nervous, but I had worked hard on my speech and had memorized the whole thing. Everyone said that I did a fine job.

Mrs. Richter took Frieda and me downtown to buy our graduation dresses. We each got to pick out the dress we wanted at Petersen's Department Store, and she said that the price didn't matter. I got a beautiful blue plaid dress with a white lace collar. It has the puffy leg o' mutton sleeves that are the most popular fashion now. We had to take it over to the seamstress at Richter's to have it taken in because the clerk said I was too thin for anything store bought to fit right. I think it looked perfect when it was done. I thanked Mrs. Richter for her kindness and generosity, but she just said that it was important for anyone from the Richter family to always look their best. I wanted to tell her that people shouldn't be judged on appearances, but instead I just wrote down my thoughts in my journal.

With love,
Emily,

*   *   *

December 4, 1898

Dear Mama and Papa Davis,

This may just be my happiest Christmas ever because I have already received the only gift that I wanted—Henry is home from the Spanish-American War. I was so worried about him during the months that he was away, and I prayed every night that he would return home safely. All my prayers have been answered.

As you know, Henry was fighting in Puerto Rico. He was part of the invasion of Puerto Rico on July 25, landing at Guanica and facing enemy soldiers right from the start. He was a part of several more battles, but he won't talk about it now that he is home. He just says that many good men died from the war, not just from canons and bullets, but from heat exhaustion and from yellow fever. I was so relieved when I read that the fighting had ended on August 12, but I didn't realize that there was still reason to worry about other dangers. Henry, along with all the others who were in Cuba or Puerto Rico, had to be quarantined for a month before they could come home. But I don't have to worry any longer because Henry is home safe and sound.

Edward and Horace Lawton graduated from high school this year too. Neither of them enlisted in the army. I'm glad that Horace stayed home because I kind of like him. He has a job now working at Pittsburgh Plate Glass Company, and of course, Ed is working at the store. They both played a lot of baseball in the summertime, and Elsie, Frieda, and I would still watch their games when they played on Sunday mornings just for fun. Horace is a pitcher for the company team too, so many of his games are too far away for me to see. Of course, it wouldn't be appropriate for me to do that anyway. But I do think that Horace liked seeing me at his Sunday morning games. Sometimes when he struck out a batter, he looked over to see if I was cheering for him. After the games, we would all walk home together, and Horace walked with us even though it was a little bit out of his way to walk by our house instead of going straight home.

In September, I started Davenport High School. It's a lot longer walk to get there, but Frieda and I walk together. Before school started, we selected our course of study. I chose the Latin Course because that will be the best preparation for becoming a teacher. Frieda chose the Commercial Course because that will be good preparation for working at the store. The high school is much bigger than the grammar school I attended. There are three floors of classrooms, and we go to a different room and teacher for each subject that we study. The teachers have so much knowledge to share with us. I still think I like history the best. Maybe I'll be a history teacher.

Carl and Jenny had a baby boy this year, and he is named Carl after his father. So now Papa Richter has two grandsons and one granddaughter. Elsie and I visit Will and Carl when we can to help with the babies. Most often we go to Louise's house so we can play with little Marie. She is two years old now, and she likes to play house with her dolls. She has so many toys that Papa thinks Louise and Henry are spoiling her. I don't think she is spoiled at all—she's just such a sweet little girl.

Papa bought a new building because he needed more space for the store. It was a big job moving everything even though the new store is just a block away from the old one. Papa said it is a better location, right next to Hansen's Hardware Store and half a block away from Petersen's, the biggest department store in Davenport.

I hope that this past year has brought much happiness to each of you as well. I always look forward to receiving your Christmas card and note letting me know what is happening in your lives and in Rockvale. I think of each of you often and remember you with love and best wishes for the New Year.

Love,
Emily

*   *   *

December 10, 1899

Dear Mama and Papa,

As Christmas nears, it is again a time for me to share with you the events of this past year. Last summer I worked at the Richter store during my school vacation. Frieda works there too, but she stayed on because she was not that interested in going back to high school. It wasn't very hard work; most of the time I just greeted the customers when they arrived and escorted them to the person who could help them. Sometimes

I helped out with paperwork. Whenever Papa Richter saw one of his friends in the store, he always introduced me to them. He would say, "This is Emily Bowers, Marie's daughter. Doesn't she look just like her mother?" Of course, they would always be polite and respond that I was just as pretty as my mother. Then Papa would embarrass me by telling them that I was just as smart as Marie too. But he didn't stop with that; he would also tell them that I was a straight A student in the Latin Course at the high school. I am proud of that, and I'm especially happy that Papa is proud of me too.

What I don't understand is why Papa doesn't think I should continue my high school education. I know he thinks it is wonderful that I'm a good student, but he just doesn't see any reason for a girl to get a high school diploma. I've told him how much I want to graduate from high school so that I can be a teacher. I wanted to enroll in the Normal Course after graduation, which is offered right at the high school. Then after one year, I could be a teacher in the Davenport schools. I've always loved school, and I love working with children too. I learned a lot taking care of Herbie, but I especially loved teaching him. He knew how to read even before he started school because I would write words on a slate and teach him to read and spell them. But Papa says that "teachers are a dime a dozen."

It was on a day near the end of summer when he told me that it was time for me to work full-time at the store instead of going to school. I was so disappointed that I almost started crying. He gave into my pleading to finish one more year, but I still felt sad about quitting school. Instead of going to work with Papa, I told him that I wanted to walk to the store, and that gave me time to think about my life. I realized that I've been very fortunate, and I owe so much to Papa Richter. I made up my mind that I will work hard at the store and make him proud of me for that too. Sometimes things don't always turn out the way you plan, but I'm going to make the best of the way things are. That way I will focus my thoughts on positive things. Papa always says, "Make the best of the hand you've been dealt," and this is a chance for me to prove that I'm able to do that.

Remember that I told you about Horace—the boy who lives in our neighborhood. He came over to our house often during the summer to visit Henry and hear all his stories about the war. Sometimes I would bring them glasses of lemonade, and they would invite me to sit with them. Even when Henry had to leave for work, Horace sometimes stayed and talked to me. We have so much in common, so there are many experiences and feelings we can share with each other. I found out that Horace is an orphan too. He doesn't remember his own father or his mother. He lived in an orphanage in New York City, but he doesn't recall that either. Do you remember how frightened I used to be of ever having to live in an orphanage? Horace came to Davenport on an orphan train when he was just four years old. He said that he has a vague memory of being on the train, but mostly he just remembers being cold and hungry. Twenty-eight of the children were taken off the train in Davenport, and that was when he was separated from his own sister. He has no idea what happened to her. He remembers that she hugged him and told him to be a good boy. I realize now how fortunate I was that you and then the Richters were willing to take all three of us girls into your homes so we could stay together. I can't imagine my life without Elsie and Maria.

Horace told me that all the children from the train were taken to a big room at St. Mary's School. The children were seated in the front, and lots of adults were standing around the room. A young woman came over and talked to him and gave him a stick of peppermint candy. That was the first time he met his sister Mary, and the first time he ever tasted candy. Peppermint is still his favorite. Mary talked her parents into adopting Horace. She was a school teacher, but since she wasn't married, she couldn't adopt him herself. Mr. and Mrs. Lawton were very old, so it was really Mary who was like a mother to him—just like Louise was a mother to Elsie, Maria, and me when we came to Davenport.

Mary married Edward Cunningham a few years later, and they moved into the house next door to the Lawtons, so she continued to take care of Horace when he was growing up. In many ways, Horace's life was harder than mine because he didn't have brothers and sisters his own age. He said that Mary made up for that by spending a lot of time with him. He even showed me a scrapbook that they made together with pictures of animals, flowers, and people that they cut out of greeting cards. Horace knows that he was very lucky to have a good home since many of the orphans were adopted by farm families who just needed more workers on their farms. Mary's husband died a few years ago, so now she must work for a living. She has a good position at a department store in Rock Island. She would have liked to go back to teaching, but women aren't allowed to teach after they get married. Maybe that's part of the reason that Papa Richter doesn't think it makes sense for a woman to spend a lot of time getting an education only to be dismissed from her job if she gets married.

Since this is my final year at the high school, I'm trying to savor every minute. I study hard to keep up my straight As even though it won't really matter now. It's still important to me to always do my best. I added some of the commercial courses to my schedule this year because I thought they might help me learn the things I need to know to help with the business. My favorite classes are still history and literature.

I hope you have been healthy and happy this past year. Best wishes for a merry Christmas to all of you. It is the dawn of a new century, and I hope that the start of the twentieth century will also begin many wonderful years ahead for each of you and all your family.

Love,
Emily

*   *   *

December 5, 1900

Dear Mama and Papa Davis,

It appears the turn of the century has also marked a turning point in my life—leaving behind my childhood days and beginning my adult life. I've been working at Richter's full-time now since my high school classes ended in June. It's not the job I would have chosen, but it can be interesting. I especially like it when I can overhear the men talking about politics and current events. One of the main topics of conversation for the men is prohibition. I think all of Papa Richter's German friends are strongly opposed to it. Most of them also supported President McKinley over William Jennings Bryan in the presidential election. There was much discussion about the Boer War in South Africa and the Boxer Rebellion in China. It's a good way for me to learn by listening to their debates and differences of opinion. Everyone was excited about the first flight of the Zeppelin in Germany. Certainly, this is the start of some amazing advances in our lives.

Some of the women talk a lot about the latest fashions or the most important social events to attend. Of course, I should know about that too so I can do a good job selling clothes, hats, and fur coats. There are plenty of women who are interested in more than fashion and the latest gossip. One day I waited on Dr. Jennie McCowen. It is an inspiration to see that women can attain such significant accomplishments. She earned a degree from the University of Iowa Medical School and has practiced medicine in Davenport for twenty years now. She also helped found a club to help young working women called Lend-A-Hand. Sometimes I stop by to listen to lectures after work. That way I feel like I'm continuing my education even if I'm not enrolled in high school. Dr. McCowen and her friend Mary Putnam are also members of the Academy of Sciences and are just as respected as any man for their research and writings in natural history and the sciences.

The best part of my day is the early morning when Papa and I have our tea together. In the summer we sit on the front porch, and in winter we sit in the library by the fire. We are both early risers, so the house is still quiet, and we talk about the store or the family or something we've read in the newspaper. Sometimes we just sit quietly. Then I think about Horace. Just after my seventeenth birthday in June, he asked Papa for permission to court me, and thankfully, Papa said yes.

Sometimes when Horace comes over, we just go for long walks together. One time we took the streetcar to Schuetzen Park way out on the west side of the city. They have a shooting park there, but neither of us have much interest in that. We do like the band concerts there and at Central Park. Central Park is my favorite because it has lovely walking paths with ponds, fountains, and bridges and the most beautiful rose garden. There's even a conservatory filled with all kinds of exotic plants. Horace loves music, and he can play the banjo and has a wonderful singing voice. When the band is playing, he quietly sings the words, and it's like he is serenading me even when there are hundreds of other people in the crowd. My favorite was when he sang "When You Were Sweet Sixteen." One hot summer Sunday afternoon, we packed a picnic lunch and rode the streetcar all the way to Suburban Island. We ate our lunch in a forested glade right at the river's edge and then took off our shoes and went wading in the river. That was the first time Horace kissed me. Don't think less of me for telling about being kissed, but I always share with you the events that are most special in my life, and certainly my first kiss was one of those.

Since I'm working all day and spending more time with Horace, I don't have as much time to visit Will or Carl or Louise. Will had another baby boy this year whom they named Rudolph. I miss seeing more of little Marie and the babies. They grow up so fast. I imagine you feel that way about Ella's children too. It's so nice that Maggie and her little ones are only a couple blocks away. I wish all of you a very merry Christmas and joyous New Year.

With love,
Emily

*   *   *

December 7, 1901

Dear Mama and Papa Davis,

This year has gone by so quickly that it is hard to believe Christmas is almost here. I always look forward to this season and to hearing from you. It is especially fun to read about Ella and Maggie's children—they are growing up so fast. Little

Maude is five years old now, and next year she'll be going to Rockvale School. Is Mr. Hutton still there? With your descriptions and stories of Maude and Johnny and Ella's three little boys, I really feel like I have come to know each of them just a little bit. I remember when Maggie and Ella took Elsie and me to wade in Oak Creek, and now I can picture all their children playing there just like we did in the summertime.

I must share with you an inspirational experience I had recently. One day Mary Putnam came into the store to invite all of us clerks to the lecture by Phoebe Sudlow at the Lend-A-Hand Club. Elsie and I decided to go because Miss Sudlow is a renowned professor at the University of Iowa—the very first female professor at the university. She was an incredible speaker. She talked about how important it was for women to pursue their goals. She said that women are as capable as men to be doctors, lawyers, professors, and businesswomen. It made me think of my mother, who came to America when she was seventeen and helped Papa Richter establish his fur store in Davenport and then moved out to the frontier in Colorado and helped my father open and run a boarding house. I know all my older brothers believe my mother was a strong and capable woman.

Miss Sudlow said that women must stand up for their rights too. She was the first female to be a public school principal—she was the principal of my grammar school, but that was before I came to Davenport. Then she was the high school principal and the first female superintendent of schools—not just first in Davenport but in the whole country. When the board of education offered her the superintendent's position, they were not going to give her the same salary as her predecessor, but she told them that if they considered her less qualified, she would accept their decision, but if they were paying her less because she was a woman, they had nothing more to talk about. That had to take a lot of courage. While she served as superintendent and later as head of the Iowa State Teachers' Association, she insisted that women's pay be equal to men's but also that women be held to the same standards. She said that equal rights also mean equal responsibilities. She said that no matter what our jobs or whatever life path we choose to follow, we must take pride in our work and always do our best. She encouraged us to get involved in the issues we believe in and always continue learning. She challenged us to work for women's right to vote. The right to vote is the most important goal for all of us. The entire audience gave her a standing ovation that lasted for many minutes.

At first, listening to Miss Sudlow, I felt disappointed in myself for not trying harder to pursue my dreams to be a teacher, but then I thought about Horace and realized that my dreams now are about marrying Horace. As much as I once wanted to be a teacher, now I want to have a family of my own. Maybe someday women will be allowed to have a teaching career and be married too, but right now we must make a choice. So even if I were a teacher, now I would choose to marry Horace. As a wife and mother, I can still follow Miss Sudlow's advice and continue to learn from every experience and to instill the values of education, equality, and responsibility in my children.

Henry was married a couple months ago to Minnie Stender. Horace and I attended the wedding together, so I couldn't help but imagine my own wedding while we were at the ceremony. Afterwards Horace said that he is going to speak to Papa Richter to ask his permission for my hand in marriage. I'm sure that Papa will give his consent because I know he likes Horace, but he also worries that Horace spends too much of his time playing baseball. That's not fair because Horace gets paid to pitch for the ball teams in the little towns surrounding Davenport. I know he doesn't make a lot of money working at Pittsburgh

Plate Glass Company, but he is very conscientious about saving as much as he can. Horace also told me that he has talked to Mr. and Mrs. Lawton about renting one of the little houses they own after we get married. So you see, I know that he is going to ask me to marry him, and I also know that I'll say yes!

I also have some news about Will before I end my letter. He bought an automobile for his family this summer. It's called an Oldsmobile, and two people can ride in it. Will drove it over to the house and gave everyone a ride around the block. You should have seen the neighbors all come out to stare at us. It looks so funny to see this carriage going down the street without horses pulling it. Will said that it can travel twenty miles per hour, but he didn't drive it that fast because he didn't want to frighten us. It's the only Oldsmobile in the whole city of Davenport, and there are only a few hundred in the whole country, but Will says that cars will be the most important means of transportation in the future. He is even thinking about quitting the fur store and going into the moving and storage business with Mr. Ewert. Will says that someday all the moving will be done by trucks instead of wagons. I know that Papa doesn't want him to leave the store, but he knows that Will is a very capable businessman with lots of experience and will be successful at any business he runs.

It was such a tragedy this year when our President McKinley was shot and killed. What a terrible thing to have happen in the United States of America, just like when President Lincoln was shot. I hope that the coming year will bring a better and happier future for all Americans. With that thought in mind, I wish you all a very merry Christmas!

Love,
Emily

*   *   *

November 29, 1902

Dear Mama and Papa,

I'm writing my annual Christmas letter early this year because December is going to be a very busy month for me. Last Christmas was the best ever because Horace asked me to marry him. It was so romantic and sweet. I think he was nervous about proposing to me. Didn't he know that I've been in love with him since I was twelve years old? It was the happiest day of my life. I wish you could meet Horace and he could meet you. I know you would like him. He says that he feels like he knows you because of all the stories I've shared with him about growing up in your home in Colorado.

We've spent a lot of time this year making plans. We decided to have the wedding in December when the house would be all decorated for Christmas. That's always one of my favorite times of the year. We'll have the ceremony right by the big candlelit tree in the parlor. Then everyone can stay for some wedding cake or Christmas cookies and fruit cake. We will even have German beer for the Richter men, Irish whiskey for the Lawton men, and tea and hot chocolate for the ladies and children. We will be renting the duplex on Ninth Street that Mr. and Mrs. Lawton own. It is just a block away from my home, a half block from his parents and across the backyard from Mary's house. We'll have three rooms on the first floor and an upstairs bedroom.

All my sisters have been a great help to me. Frieda is going to help me pick out my dress, and Elsie has been practicing on my hair so she can fix it in the latest Gibson Girl style. Louise said that she would bake the wedding cake, but Maria and Alma must take care of little Marie so that she won't be distracted while doing such an important task. Marie is six years old now, so she'll probably want to help, but she'd just get in the way. Trudy is seven, but she's a little tomboy and has no interest in being in the kitchen; she would much rather be following Herbie around the neighborhood and climbing trees.

Horace and I have already received some wedding gifts, and I just must tell you about a couple that really have a special meaning to me. Henry and Minnie gave us a framed engraving called *Pharaoh's Horses*. He said that the wild horses were to remind me of my childhood days in Colorado and of all the days I spent visiting Papa's horses in the stable that first summer I lived in Davenport. Horace's sister, Mary Cunningham, gave us a beautiful patchwork crazy quilt that she quilted and embroidered herself eighteen years ago, the year that Horace was adopted, so you can see why it is so special. Every time I was at her house, I admired it. I never tired of looking at all the intricate pictures and embroidery—it reminds me of the pictures in the scrapbook that Mary helped Horace make when he was just a little boy. Already I feel like Mary considers me truly a member of her family.

I am happy looking forward to beginning my life with Horace, but I really miss having a mother who would talk to me about love and marriage. There is so much I would like to ask my mother about her life and the decisions she made. Louise told me several years ago that she left Papa Richter because he had been unfaithful. Papa Richter is so good to us that it is hard for me to imagine he would have been unfaithful to her, especially because I know he loved my mother—he told me that when I first came to live here. I understand now why he never wanted to talk about it. I wish I could ask her about all these things.

Mrs. Richter was kind to take me into her home and raise me with her own family, and I cannot fault her for anything. I'm grateful that I have lived in a good home with a caring family for the past ten years. My sisters are wonderful, and we all love each other so much, but it's still not the same as having a mother. More than anything, I wish my mother could share my joy now. I like to think that she knows Elsie, Maria, and I have had a happy life. My papa and Papa Richter always told me how much my mother loved me, but I do wish that I could remember her and remember being loved by her. Sometimes I feel like there is a hole in my heart that could only be filled by a mother's love. Mama Davis, you were a loving mother to me when I was little, so I should not feel like anything is missing from my life. Besides, this is not a time to be thinking of any sad thoughts. I will think only about Horace and our love for each other and pray that we will always be happy together and that we will have children to love. There is so much that I can look forward to.

With all my love and best wishes for a wonderful Christmas and the happiest of new years to all of you,

Emily

Part 2
Marie and Traugott

July 13, 1904

Mrs. Horace Lawton
932 W. Ninth Street
Davenport, Iowa

Dear Mrs. Lawton:

Please accept my condolences for the loss of your stepfather. We were all saddened by his death in June. He will be greatly missed by many in this community.

As administrator of the estate of Traugott Richter and in accordance with his instructions, I am delivering to you the enclosed packet of documents. Mr. Richter brought this packet to my law office in April of 1903 and instructed me to give it to you in person after the time of his death.

I have had the privilege of serving as Mr. Traugott Richter's attorney for the past twenty years, and as such, I prepared his last will and testament, advised him on personal and business matters, and was entrusted with keeping both his personal and legal documents. The formal reading of his will occurred yesterday at the home of his widow, Mrs. Wilhelmina Richter. Mr. Richter's business interests were left to his natural children, with Carl serving as president of T. Richter and Sons. His personal assets were placed in the control of his oldest son, William Richter, who was named trustee of the estate. His home at 1025 Ninth Street was left to his widow, Wilhelmina, and maintenance of the home will come from the estate. Traugott did specifically state that all his natural children as well as the children of Marie Richter Bowers were to be allowed to live in that home if they desired to do so. Rest assured that your sisters, Elsie and Maria, may remain living there until they marry or decide to live elsewhere. There were no further bequests to you or to your sisters in Traugott's will. However, there is a trust account for you, Elsie, and Maria at the German American Bank. Mr. Carl will be in touch with you soon regarding its distribution.

Yours truly,
Ernest Stebbens

*   *   *

January 16, 1903

Dearest Emily,

The time has come for me to share my memories with you, and I have chosen to write this letter to you since it is too painful for me to talk about many of these things. I'm not going to give this memoir to you now because I couldn't bear it if you resented me for the things I did. So I will enclose this in an envelope, which I will entrust to my lawyer and friend, Ernest Stebbens, and you will receive it from him after my death.

Before I begin the story, I must first explain my will. I revised it just this last year because William no longer wants to be directly involved with the daily operation of T. Richter and Sons Fur Store. Carl, Henry, and Edward are involved and want to stay involved with the store. By the time you read this letter, you will know that I have left all of my estate to my direct descendants. William will serve as the executor of my personal estate. The store will be managed by my sons, who will serve as officers. Herbert will also be involved in the management if he wishes after he is grown. Louise, Frieda, Alma, and Trudy also are part owners of the business. Our home on Ninth Street has been left to my wife Wilhelmina, with the stipulation that she is always to provide living quarters for you and your sisters if any of you wish to stay there. The necessary living expenses for Wilhelmina and all my children who are still under the age of twenty-one and maintenance of the home will be provided from my estate according to William's discretion. Emily, as long as I am alive, I will do anything I can for you whenever you need me, and the same is true for Elsie and Maria. I have loved the three of you just as much as I love my own flesh and blood—in so many ways I do consider you my own. After my death, my obligation is to provide for my dependent children and ensure that their futures are secure. I must also make sure that Wilhelmina will be cared for financially. In the early years of our marriage, I was not always the most loving or attentive husband, but I did and will continue to provide for her financial well-being. I hope you understand and forgive me for not including you, Elsie, and Maria as heirs of my estate. However, I have kept a separate account for many years at the German-American Bank from which my banker, Mr. Carl, paid your mother a monthly stipend for the support of Will, Carl, Louise, and Henry. I have taken that money, which they no longer need, and set up a trust account for you, Elsie, and Maria. I instructed Mr. Carl privately to close out the account following my death with a lump sum payment divided equally between the three of you. Mr. Stebbens is aware of this arrangement, which has been kept separate from my estate, so there will be no chance that anything you girls receive would be contested. If you do not receive this payment in a timely manner, please inform Mr. Stebbens so he can facilitate the transfer of money to you from the account.

On this cold, wintry day I have decided to sit down at my desk in the library and begin the story that I promised to tell you last summer. I've told the boys not to expect me at the store so that I can begin this letter to you. I know it will take some time to finish, but it is time at least to begin. This is not an easy task for me as you will understand when you read it. I will apologize in advance if some parts of this story seem indelicate or inappropriate, but you are a married woman now, so I can say things that I wouldn't have said to you last summer. I will make this promise: I will tell you the whole story of your mother's life with me with total honesty and openness. I want you to learn about my life with Marie from my perspective as well as hers and not versions told by others after I'm gone.

I will always treasure those mornings we would sit on the porch drinking tea and watching the sky turn from pale gray to blue. We enjoyed seeing the rays of sunshine penetrate the trees and sparkle on the morning dew. It was always so peaceful then before the rest of the family was awake. You often asked me to tell you more about Marie, but it was hard for me to talk about her. It made me sad to talk about the good times I shared with Marie, and it was impossible for me to tell you about the bad times.

Some mornings you would ask me what was on my mind, and I told you I was thinking about my plans for the day ahead. Honestly, when I was sitting next to you, I was thinking about Marie. You brought back all my memories of Marie; you are so much like her—beautiful, bright, and possessing great inner strength. You've always been mature for your age, probably a result of losing both your parents at such a young age and watching over your sisters. Marie was also so young—only seventeen when she left home and made the daunting journey to America to become my wife.

Emily, I realized during our morning conversations that you would have been a wonderful teacher, and I was wrong not to let you pursue your dream. Just like Marie, you knew what you wanted when you were sixteen, but I let my head rule my heart, thinking that you would make a better living working at the store. I see now that I was also selfish—I wanted your company at the store. Louise, Frieda, and Elsie seemed happy when they were working there, but it wasn't best for you. You would have been much happier as a teacher. You were always so good with Herbert—and that was no easy job! And Marie would have wanted that for you too—especially to complete your education. But now you have begun a home of your own, and someday soon I'm sure that home will also be filled with children. Horace is a good man who loves you dearly. I hope all the years of your life will be filled with happiness.

With that said, I will begin my story:

When the time came for me to decide what I wanted to do with my life, I had two goals: first to learn a trade and then to immigrate to America. At the age of seventeen, I moved from Berlin to Leipzig to become a furrier. My uncle Johann Wolf had a successful fur business and was willing to take me in as an apprentice. It was an excellent learning experience with a highly skilled furrier, and I was even provided opportunities to make fur coats and hats for European royalty. I was fortunate in that I could also live in my uncle's home and thus save what little I made to advance my second goal—coming to America. When my apprenticeship was complete, my uncle would have been happy to give me a job, but he had sons who would inherit the business, and I wanted to be on my own. I knew that the greatest opportunities for success were in America. In 1865, when the War Between the States was ending and many people were moving to the western states, the time was right. Like many other young Germans, I also wanted to get away from Prussia and the wars that were sure to come under the leadership of Bismarck. I was not willing to sacrifice my life for his goals to create an empire, and thus I headed to America.

It only took a couple weeks to cross the Atlantic on a steamship from Hamburg to New York. I traveled in steerage because that was all I could afford, and despite my bedraggled appearance when I disembarked at Castle Garden, I was allowed immediate entrance into the country because I was healthy and possessed a skill that would provide an income for me. It didn't take long for me to find employment in New York, and I stayed there for six months while I saved my money for a train ticket to Chicago. On the way, I met a fellow German returning from a visit to his homeland, and he offered me employment in his carriage shop in Dixon, Illinois. Of course, that wasn't the job I desired, but any work would do until I could save more money and invest in some furs. While working there, one of the clients complimented me on my fur hat. I told him that I would sell it to him since I could make another as soon as I could afford to buy some furs. He suggested that when I was ready, he would be happy to help me set up shop in some vacant store space he owned not far away in Geneseo. As soon as I had saved seventy-five dollars, I went back to Chicago, bought some furs, and then traveled to Geneseo. The next two years were busy, but I missed my family and the active life I had enjoyed in both Leipzig and Berlin. I wrote often to my parents, and they were pleased to hear about my success but also concerned that my life was lacking companionship. I told them that I wasn't satisfied with my life in Geneseo and hoped to someday move on again to a larger town located farther to the west, Davenport, Iowa. There were many things about Davenport that attracted me. It was known as the Queen of the West. There was superior transportation due to its location on the Mississippi River and on the railroad. In fact, the first railroad bridge to cross the river connected Rock Island, Illinois, and Davenport. With the river, I would be able to access furs from the northern traders, and with the railroad, I could get furs from wholesale businesses in the east. Perhaps, the most convincing attribute, however, was the existence of a large German population. I knew that would provide not only many potential customers but also a source of companionship.

I must stop for today and get to the store. I'm sure by this time Carl or Henry has telephoned the house, wondering what happened to me.

Saturday, January 24, 1903

Hopefully, I can manage some time alone this morning to continue and get to the important part of this narrative, your mother, Marie.

Reading my letters, my parents worried about my loneliness and thought that what I really needed was a wife, and they had a young German girl in mind. She was the daughter of the Schmidt family, their neighbors in Berlin. Of course, I remembered the family and vaguely remembered Marie as a feisty and cute young girl. However, she was only fifteen when I left Germany at the age of twenty-one, so I hadn't paid much attention to her. My parents told me that she was attractive and intelligent and, at seventeen, of marriageable age. Apparently, she was also fascinated by the accounts she heard about life in America—first from her older sister Ruth, who had immigrated with her husband to Des Moines, Iowa, a few years earlier, and now from the stories my parents related about me. She did also remember me; maybe she even had a schoolgirl crush on the older neighbor boy. Her parents were evidently amenable to the idea of an arrangement between us. They were, after all, friends of my parents, and they also heard the tales of my success in America—perhaps tales that were slightly exaggerated by proud parents. Marie's interest in this arrangement was probably enhanced by her desire to live in America—she saw it as a land of opportunity for women as well as men.

Marie and I started corresponding, and I could see that she was interested in all aspects of my life in America. Her questions and comments were evidence of her intelligence. She also told me how she hated leaving school when she finished eighth grade—she felt that she had so much more to learn. But she wasn't the least bit interested in learning the things she was expected to do at home—cooking, baking, sewing, and all the typical household chores. She told me that she would sit outside the parlor when her father had friends to visit. She would pretend to be working on her embroidery but was really just listening as the men discussed business and politics. Her mother would send her up to her room if she was found out, but Marie thought her father secretly appreciated her interest. She loved reading and had read many of Shakespeare's plays and of course the works of Goethe and Schiller. Now she was focusing on learning English.

Our families agreed that when I could send the money to pay for her passage, Marie should travel to America, where I would meet her in New York and accompany her to Geneseo. I would arrange accommodations for her at a reputable boarding house. Fortunately, there was a boarding house in town that was run by a widowed woman from my church. She would be able to provide a room and would be a suitable chaperone for Marie until we were married. She also wrote to Marie's parents to assure them that Marie would be in safe company. Knowing Marie as I do now, she would not be a woman who would let anyone take advantage of her. In fact, my parents had cautioned me that Marie was a strong-willed young woman, but they also thought her strength would be an asset to me in America. I discovered that trait quickly for myself. I was looking forward to being able to converse in my native language again, but Marie soon informed me that she wanted to practice her English when we were together. She said that if she was going to live in America, she was going to learn the language as soon as possible. She was not going to rely on a husband to express her opinions or converse with neighbors for her. I admired her determination.

I thought today would be a good chance to write undisturbed, but Herbie is interrupting my train of thought, begging me to take him ice skating at Suburban Park. He seems to think the ice will melt if we don't go immediately.

February 7, 1903

As I reread my last paragraph, I realized that I was getting ahead of myself. In September of 1867, Marie arrived in New York. I was waiting as she came off the boat from Castle Garden. I did not recognize Marie at first. She was quite petite and from a distance looked very young. In addition, my parents had described her as attractive, but the woman I saw was truly beautiful to me. I wondered at my parents' evaluation—could this be the strong young woman who wanted to leave a comfortable life in Germany and move to the frontier of America with a man she hardly knew? But I quickly learned that Marie had a strength of character not evidenced by her lovely, demure appearance; she was enthusiastic about everything that she had thus far experienced and anxious to see and learn all she could about her new home. I did learn afterward that Marie had insisted before leaving Germany that if she was unhappy with me or the way in which she was treated, she had enough money with her to travel to Des Moines where she could live with Ruth and her family until she could manage to arrange to return to Germany. Fortunately, that never became an issue. I loved her enthusiasm, her interest in my life and business, and the way she immediately assumed her place as my equal. I could see that she would truly be a partner in my life. By the time we reached Geneseo, I had fallen in love. It was only two months after arriving in Geneseo that we were married. I do believe that Marie was as much in love with me as I was with her.

Emily, perhaps I'm repeating myself, but when you were seventeen, my heart ached just looking at you because you reminded me of my Marie at that age. You were lovely, intelligent, and interested in learning just like Marie. I'm sure your mother would not have let me dictate her future, but you were always an obedient and respectful daughter—you would never have considered arguing with me when I insisted that you come to work at the store.

Prior to my marriage, I also made several trips to Davenport, just twenty miles away, to check out the possibilities for starting a fur business there. Marie wanted to know every detail when I would return from these missions. She was as excited as I was when I told her that I had found a space to rent on Second Street in an up-and-coming business location. On November 7, 1867, we were married. She insisted on accompanying me when I went back to sign the contract to lease the store and to look for a place for us to live. Our honeymoon was spent at the Germania House, a lovely hotel near the river on Second Street. We found a flat in the German neighborhood in West Davenport. We had so much to be thankful for when we celebrated our first Thanksgiving together in America, but most of all I was thankful for this amazing woman who was now my wife and the love of my life. Before year's end, we had moved to Davenport.

During those early years, our time was consumed with the store. Marie wanted to help, and I quickly discovered that her help was invaluable. She was much better at keeping the books than I was. Things were going well by the time our first son, Willie, was born. We were such proud parents, and he was a wonderful baby. Marie stayed at home after his birth, but I still brought the store records home, and she would check over the accounts in the evenings.

Life was even busier, but we both enjoyed working hard and building our future together. Two years later, Carl was born and a year after that Louise. Willie was the perfect big brother. He always wanted to help and do whatever he could to please us. Carl was very bright, just like his older brother, and athletic too. Louise was a perfect little lady and so easygoing. When she wasn't at her mother's side, she liked to tag along with the boys and play with them. By the time Louise was born, we had moved to a larger home—the first that we owned. It was a frame home with three bedrooms on the second floor. Marie was a loving mother, and she enjoyed her time with the children, but she didn't much enjoy keeping house. Fortunately, the store was doing well, with much credit going to Marie, and I was able to hire a young German girl to come help with the cleaning and cooking a couple days of the week.

Our life was happy. We even took our three children back to visit our families in Germany. It was such a wonderful time for us—a chance to reunite with our families and friends and to give our parents a chance to meet our three wonderful children. Willie and Carl both knew enough German that they could communicate with our families. We were so proud of them.

Then came days of sorrow. When Marie was expecting our fourth child, she was very sick. The doctors were afraid she might lose the baby, so they ordered her to stay in bed. Our little girl, Nonnie, was born very weak and only survived a couple of days. Her death devastated both of us. We tried to do our best to hide our sadness from our three little ones and keep our lives as normal as possible. Soon we were expecting our fifth child, and life seemed to be good again. Little Marie was a healthy baby at birth. Then the worst happened again. Baby Marie came down with scarlet fever, and after weeks of struggle, she died. I don't know how either of us made it through those next few weeks.

During the months that followed, a time when we needed each other more than ever, we both pulled away into our own personal grief. We no longer seemed to be able to share our feelings. Marie insisted on going back to work at the store. When she was at home, she concentrated all her attention on our three older children who were seven, five, and four years of age. I admit that I spent too much time at the old Turner Hall with my friend Karl, drinking a stein or two of beer, smoking cigars, and playing pinochle. Of course, I was also at the store but involved in my own responsibilities. On Saturdays I took Willie and Carl to the Northwest Turnverein for their gymnastic classes and then would go back to the store to work until they were ready to be picked up. Marie spent her time with little Louise. After attending services at the Lutheran church, Sundays were a family day, but somehow the children kept us so busy we didn't have time to talk to each other.

Now I must pause again while I listen to Trudy practice her recitation for school.

March 14, 1903

Time has slipped away from me again. I can't believe it has been a month since I last sat down to write to you. Hopefully, today I can accomplish more.

Getting back to our troubles—I thought that I needed to do something to make Marie happy again, so I conceived the idea of building a beautiful house for her. I thought that a big home with lots of bedrooms would symbolize our hopes for a future with more children to fill up the space with laughter and happiness. With that in mind, I had something to occupy every spare minute of my time and all my thoughts as well. On my way home from work, I used to study the architecture of the grand homes on the bluff along Seventh Street. There were so many lovely Victorian homes, but my favorite was the Italianate style with its high tower and tall windows. I started looking for an accomplished builder who could build a home that would be elegant both outside and inside. I also started looking for sites. I knew that I wanted to be close to town but on the bluff overlooking the city. I also wanted land with a lot of trees to protect the house from the winter winds and keep it cool in the summer heat. I found six acres of land bordering Marquette Street. We would have a winding drive up the hill and build the house on the crest.

The house I built for Marie was a brick Italianate mansion with ten rooms on the two main floors—including six bedrooms upstairs. The entrance was through a marble-floored foyer that separated two parlors each with their own marble fireplace. The dining room had a beautiful stained glass window; the walls were paneled in oak with oak beams in the ceiling as well. An elegant chandelier hung from the sculptured plaster ceiling. The library also had stained glass windows, built-in walnut bookcases, and a corner fireplace—I imagined that would be Marie's favorite room since she always loved to read. From the foyer, an intricately carved staircase led to the upstairs bedrooms. There were additional rooms on the third floor for servants. Perhaps my favorite space was the tower room with its windows on all four sides. I envisioned the two of us spending our evenings there, enjoying the lights of the city after all our children were in bed.

We moved into the house even before it was completely finished. Now we needed the help of our maid, Wilhelmina, on a full-time basis, and she moved into one of the attic rooms along with a nursemaid for the children. Marie still wanted to work at the store. So every day I would leave at noon to go home and supervise the work that was still being done on the house. Wilhelmina would be there working hard to clean up after the workmen completed one room and had moved on to another. It was an endless and thankless job. I felt sorry for asking her to do so many extra jobs, so I would invite her to eat lunch with me. She loved the house and raved about what a wonderful place it was. She listened to my stories about the design and building of the house and admired all that I had accomplished. She seemed to appreciate everything and showed such interest in listening to every story I told about the construction of the house. I was flattered by her respect and admiration.

Emily, I tell you this not to justify my actions but to explain what can happen even when a love is as strong as my love for your mother. A marriage requires more than love; it takes hard work, communication, patience, respect, and sometimes even sacrifice. I was too caught up in my own needs to see what Marie needed from me. And Marie didn't recognize my need for her. Anyway, Wilhelmina was there and willing to give me what I needed—attention, admiration, and herself. I selfishly accepted. I do not want you to attach any blame on Mina; I am totally responsible for the mistakes I made. Mina was from a poor German immigrant family and had been forced into domestic service at a very young age. It is no wonder that she was in awe of my home and my standing in the community. I took advantage of her admiration of me, and I will be forever sorry for my weakness.

At no time during my affair with Mina did I stop loving Marie. Yet, I realize now that Wilhelmina thought I loved her. She probably imagined we would leave Davenport together, posing as man and wife, and I would start another fur business in some western town far away from any of the gossip that would surround us in Davenport. Did I ever use the word *love* when I was with her? I do not remember that I did, but I know that I was attracted to her and somehow managed to justify my actions in my own mind. I swear to you that I never made any promises to her because Marie was the only woman I truly loved and desired as a wife.

When Marie told me that we were going to have another baby, she seemed so happy for the first time in several years. I told Mina that our affair had to stop immediately, but in an effort to be kind, I said that I wouldn't expect her to leave her job. She would be welcome to stay on until she could find more satisfactory employment. That's when she told me that she also was going to have a baby, and I was the father. I had no reason to doubt her. Suffice it to say, Mina was a virgin when I first made love to her, so there was no reason to doubt that I had fathered her baby. I still thought I could buy my way out of the awful situation. I told her that I would give her whatever money she needed to leave town and give birth to the baby, but she would have to put the child up for adoption. (I shudder now when I think that I could have lost my son Edward.) I'm sure that I sound cold-hearted, but my only thought at the time was of Marie, our children, and keeping my terrible secret from her.

Mina cried and begged me not to desert her. She said that she loved me. I was guilt-ridden but adamant that there would be no future for us; I was not in love with her. I truly thought that she would do whatever I asked of her. I assumed that she would willingly take the generous amount of money I offered and abide by my directives. I didn't realize that she was determined to convince Marie of our affair. Apparently she understood Marie better than I. She was gambling on the chance that Marie would leave me once she found out about the affair—how right she was.

She went to Marie to tell the whole sordid story. She told Marie all the details from our first embrace to the methods I used to contrive time alone with her during those long lunch breaks I took at home. At first, Marie did not believe her because she couldn't imagine that I would do such a thing. She accused her of being a liar and much worse. She thought Wilhelmina was trying to manipulate her in order to get what she wanted—a wealthy husband and a father for her baby. But Marie's angry words did not intimidate Wilhelmina. Once again, I underestimated the strength of the women in my life. She suggested that Marie ask the workmen or the nursemaid if they had seen the two of us disappear into her bedroom after our lunches together. She also claimed that she was prepared to have her baby and raise it in Davenport, telling everyone in town that I was the father. She assured Marie that I had already promised to support her and the baby, so by that fact alone, I had admitted my guilt.

That night Marie met me at the door when I returned from the store. Her face was streaked with tears. She said that the children had all been sent to stay the night with friends so we could talk. Then she told me everything that Wilhelmina had said, and Wilhelmina had not left out any of the details. Marie asked if it was true. I will admit that my first instinct was to deny it, but I couldn't add lying to Marie to my list of transgressions. If Marie found out I was lying, as she likely would, there would be no way I could ever regain her trust. So I admitted my wrongdoing but insisted that I loved only her and begged for forgiveness. I foolishly believed that our marriage would survive because wives just didn't leave their husbands and the security of marriage. Divorce was unheard of in those times, especially in our circle of friends and associates. Certainly other men I knew had been unfaithful to their wives, and some even kept mistresses. It was just something that many women accepted as preferable to being labeled a divorcee. I knew Marie would be angry if she found out about the affair, but I thought she would forgive me for the sake of our family and her love for me. I promised to always be faithful to her in the future, and I did intend to keep that promise. I never wanted to be the person capable of causing so much anguish to the woman I loved.

Again, I obviously didn't understand Marie. She said that I could not possibly cause such hurt to someone I loved and still claim to love her. Everything I had done and said was deceitful, and she would never trust me again no matter what I said. I had humiliated her in front of the staff at home and in our business—and not only that, but soon most of Davenport would also know of my weakness and how I had disgraced both of us. I had destroyed any love or respect she felt for me; she could never in a lifetime forget it or forgive me.

Marie told me to get out of our house immediately, and the next morning, she sent a telegram to her sister in Des Moines telling her that she was on her way with the children. She bought the train tickets for the following day. She told our children that they would be going on a trip to visit their cousins in Des Moines because their Papa was going to be away on business for a while. She allowed me to come back to kiss them all goodbye so they wouldn't have concerns about leaving.

April 11, 1903

Emily, spring has finally arrived. I'm sitting at the desk, looking out at the trees with their fresh green leaves and the daffodils and tulips just poking out of the earth. The sun is shining today, and that is my favorite part of spring—finally seeing blue skies and sunshine after our long, gray winters. I am reminded of those sweet spring days when you and I would sit on the porch talking together before going to the store. I couldn't continue with this account on those gray days in winter because the outcome of this story still breaks my heart. But I promised you the whole truth, so I will continue:

I followed Marie to Des Moines the very next day. I still had hope that I would be able to beg her forgiveness and convince her to come back to me. I couldn't even imagine my life without Marie and our children. When I arrived, I went straight to her sister Ruth's home and asked to speak to Marie. It took a lot of convincing to even get in the front door. The children were all out playing on the farm, so Marie led me into the parlor and asked Ruth for privacy. None of my entreaties made any difference to Marie; I had never seen her face so hardened. Her heart had turned to stone, and the only feeling she had for me was hatred. When I asked what I could do to earn her forgiveness, she told me that the only thing I could do was to give her a divorce as soon as possible. Finally, I realized that there was no going back, so I asked about our children. What would happen to them? Emily, you don't have children yet, but when you do, you will understand how heart-wrenching that was. To lose Marie broke my heart; to lose my children too—that pain is indescribable. Marie said that in time we would talk about it, but she couldn't deal with any decisions yet. Eventually we did arrange a plan so that Will and Carl could come for a visit in the summers when school was out. The baby was yet to be born, so it wouldn't even know me. She also said that she wanted Will and Carl to learn the business when they were older so we would make arrangements by letter once the time was right. She would allow the boys and Louise to receive my letters, and I must somehow convince them that I loved them, but for the time being, they must stay with her. I know Marie's only concern was the children. She did not ever want to see me again. Marie's Castle was now nothing but a symbol of her heartbreak; she would never return.

I cried on the trip home. I'm sure other passengers on that train must have wondered about my sanity. By the time I reached Davenport, I had decided that I would grant Marie her wish and file for the divorce. It seemed like my only option. I would ask Wilhelmina to marry me to give her baby a name and a home. What else could I do?

Mina accepted my proposal, and we were married by a justice of the peace as soon as the final divorce papers were signed. It was not a happy occasion as weddings should be, but I know that Mina still held out hope that we would have a good life together, and I would come to love her. Neither of us wanted to live in Marie's Castle, but I promised her that I would build another beautiful, big home with a view of the city. Although the castle wasn't totally finished yet, I found a buyer immediately. He was a business associate, and as part of the sale, we acquired his much smaller home where we lived until the new house on Ninth Street was built.

As you know, after Marie remarried your father the following year, she and James moved to Denver. But she still arranged for the boys to come and visit each summer. James would take them by train to Ruth's house near Des Moines, and I would pick them up there and take them to Davenport. I corresponded with them regularly—as much as you can correspond with children who were still so young. Marie sent me a photograph of Henry and said that he was a sweet baby. I did not actually see him until he was six, when I went to Denver to get Will and Carl. Marie wrote me when she knew she was dying, and I went back to Denver to get both Louise and Henry. Your father James was always very cordial to me. He loved all of Marie's children but accepted letting them go as they were my flesh and blood children, and he knew the pain of losing one's own child.

In the years following Marie's death, our children kept in touch with your father James. He, after all, had been an important part of their lives when they were young. Early in 1892, they received the sad news that James had a large tumor. His health was failing rapidly. He told them that when he could no longer manage on his own, he would return to live with the Davises and you girls in Rockvale. By early March, he said that he had lost much weight and didn't have the strength to live alone—he was on his way to Rockvale. Will came to me to discuss the situation. He was concerned about your welfare. He remembered Rockvale and described a coal-mining town that had many more saloons than churches and many more rough men than refined women. We knew the Davises were good people, and as long as your father was alive, he would be looking out for you too, but it was not an environment where Will thought his young sisters should grow up. He said that you would be better off with all of us in Davenport. I certainly agreed with that. I also knew that finally I would have a chance to atone in a small way for my past deeds. So I informed Mina of my plans and wrote a letter to James, begging him to let the three of you come to live with me and their brothers and sister in Davenport. I said all that I could to convince him that it would be best for the three of you. I realized that I could not go to talk to him in person as there would be no reason for him to trust me, but he would trust Will. So Will arrived in Rockvale in April, just two weeks before your father passed away. He carried my letter and all the ideas we had discussed to convince James to let you come to Davenport. I thank God that he was successful.

April 12, 1903

So, dear Emily, I have concluded my story of Marie and our marriage. Before I close the letter, however, I must add a few more of my thoughts and hopes. When you have read this, I hope that you can still remember me with love in your heart and forgive me for the many mistakes that I made in my life. For years I suffered from my guilt and from Marie's unwillingness to forgive me, and I couldn't take the chance that you would feel the same as her. Just please remember that I truly loved your mother and you and your sisters. At the end of her life, she had forgiven me, and that made my life more bearable. It was your presence along with your sisters in my home that brought such happiness to my life once again. You gave me a second chance to prove my love for your mother.

When Marie wrote to ask me to take Louise and Henry back to Davenport, she also wrote about her feelings towards me as well as offering me her forgiveness. She wrote in German because she was still more comfortable using her native language, especially when she wanted to ensure precise communication. I have translated her letter and am enclosing it with the hope that Marie's own words will convince you that she did love me once and recognized that I never stopped loving her. She even apologized for her part in ending our marriage, but I never blamed her in any way for the decision she made. Even though at the end of her life Marie could acknowledge she still cared for me, that in no way diminished the love she felt for your father. I am thankful that she could find happiness again and grateful to your father for making that possible.

Mina and I have had a good life together and five wonderful children of our own. I can't imagine my life without any of them. I do not deserve so many blessings in my life. I loved two beautiful women who were wonderful wives to me. I have had the privilege of raising twelve amazing children. I cannot be prouder of Will, Carl, Louise, and Henry. As I said before, you, Elsie, and Maria brought new light back into my life. Edward has been a joy to me since the day of his birth—his happy smile and outgoing personality charmed all who knew him. Now he is following in the footsteps of Carl and Henry and taking a major role in the store both as a businessman and a furrier. Freida and Alma were wonderful children and are now lovely and thoughtful women. Herbie was always the most challenging of my children, but you were able to manage him better than any of the rest of us. I think he knew that he could always count on your love. Trudy is still just a child, the same age now as you were when you came to live with us, but she shows promise of being just as bright as all her brothers and sisters.

Emily, you have always been so respectful of your stepmother, and I pray that this letter will not in any way affect your appreciation of her part in taking you and your sisters into her home. When she married me, she certainly didn't anticipate the addition to our family of seven children who were not her own.

You and your sisters had been raised by your mother and father to always be polite, respectful, and kind, so you were certainly never a burden to Wilhelmina. For me, it was a joy having you live with us. Emily, I would destroy this letter today if I thought it would change the way you regard Wilhelmina, but I know you well enough to be confident that you would never be disrespectful or unkind to anyone.

Emily, every word I've written is with the deepest gratitude for all that you are to me,

With abiding love,
Papa Richter

P.S. Marie's letter written to me three months before her death in 1887 is enclosed.

*   *   *

Denver, May 14, 1887

My Dear Traugott,

I hope you don't mind that I write "My Dear" again after seven years apart because it is important that you know I still care for you and appreciate what a good father you are to our children. There is so much that I must say about our life together, but first, I should write about our children. I have so cherished the letters that I've received these past months from Willie and Carl, and I will write to them soon. Your letter expressing concerns and prayers for my health was so much appreciated. Now, however, I must face the inevitability of death and make plans for my children.

As you heard from Willie, I have been unusually tired for a couple months now, but with the onset of fevers, I finally visited a doctor. He said that I most certainly had consumption and will not recover although he cannot predict how long I might linger. He suggested that I begin now to make arrangements for my family. I pray for the strength to face the weeks ahead with courage and to have the time to express my love to all my family as well as my hopes and dreams for each of them.

You offered in your letter that Louise and Henry could return to live with you and your family while I am convalescing, and James and I now agree that would be best for them. It would be good if you could come soon. They have been such a light in my life during all my darkest hours, but now it is time for me to think about their welfare and their future. In a few years, Henry would have returned to Davenport to learn the business just like Willie and Carl, but it is so hard for me to send him away when he is only seven. They are both such intelligent children; they have done well in school, and I have tried to provide extra challenges in arithmetic, but my English is still not much help for them with their reading and writing. I have also tried to keep them familiar with our native German language, so hopefully they will not be too far behind their classmates in Davenport. Of course, we speak English in our home since that is James's native language, and it helps me to become more proficient too, but my spelling is poor. I know the schools in Davenport are excellent, and Louise and Henry will receive a good education there.

May 15

I needed to rest but can now continue. It will break my heart to send Louise and Henry away, but this time I must put aside my selfish desires and do what is best for them. Please come to Denver to get them so they won't have to ride the train alone—I couldn't bear to think of them traveling alone, and James refuses to leave me now even for a short time. I fear that Louise and Henry will not want to leave either, but I will try to make them understand. Your kind letters to Louise over the years helped her to remember you, and Henry knows you too from the stories he's heard from his brothers. Certainly, Willie and Carl will help them adjust to their new home. I grieved when I sent the two of them away, but now I recognize that it was fortunate they have had this time with you and your family and have already adjusted to that change in their lives.

Louise has been such a help to me during my illness. She has taken over the preparation of all our dinners when she comes home from school—and her only twelve years old. When Henry comes home, he plays with Emily and Elsie. By the end of each day, I am so tired even though I've accomplished little with my time. We are fortunate to have a kind neighbor, Louise Lauche, who stops by every day to help. She is only twenty-two but has been like a mother to baby Maria. James and I have yet so much to decide on what will be best for our three girls when I'm gone.

I am thankful that Louise and Henry have you to raise them and to care for them along with Willie and Carl. It is right that they should live with you, their own father, rather than with James even though James has loved them and has been a good stepfather. You may have heard that James lost his first wife in childbirth and gave up his baby daughter, so I think he always looked at Louise as the daughter he had lost. Everyone loves Henry—he is such a serious and responsible little boy—both smart and kind. Louise and Henry will flourish in the environment that you can provide as soon as they become accustomed to the change in their lives.

Willie and Carl have been happy with you and enjoy their involvement in the store—they have learned much already. I know they are hard workers, but they also want to repay your kindness in taking them into your family. Louise and Henry are young and need a mother's love and influence. This will not be easy for Wilhelmina as I'm sure she must resent the way I treated her. Please, ask her to forgive me for the shameful way I spoke to her and to treat our children kindly. They are such good children, and I will admonish them to always be respectful to her—I know they will. I also know how much you love them, and they will need to know that too. You must also remind them often how very much I loved them.

Writing all of this has sapped my strength and my emotions, so I will rest and continue when I feel renewed. It does help that I can write to you in German so I don't have to concern myself with spelling and grammar.

May 18

I must continue so that I can get this letter posted. I am indebted for your financial help over the years. You sent more than the expected expenses needed to provide for our four children. I know that was from the goodness of your heart. Then you continued to send the same amount even after Willie and Carl had returned to Davenport. Each year I set aside some of the money to save enough to buy property, and this past year, we were able to purchase three little lots and build a home for ourselves along with two others we can rent out. I am glad we chose to do that rather than building a bigger house. The rent we receive on the little homes will help James afford someone to care for the girls.

As a woman, I had no legal right to any of your money. I believe that you did appreciate the part I played in starting up the store and running the business operations. So I felt that you intended that some of the money you sent could be spent on my family. Otherwise, making ends meet would have been a struggle. I do not want you to think that my life has been unhappy. James may not have been as successful at business as you, but he was successful in life—recognizing the joys of each day and cherishing his family. I realize now, as my life is coming to an end, that it was the love of my family that mattered most.

I am grateful that the Richter Store has been such a success. When Willie and Carl returned from their summers in Davenport, they were full of stories about the store and how respected you are in the city of Davenport. They told me about your beautiful, big home with so many rooms—I can picture the location on Ninth Street. That is quite a change from my tiny house in Denver. I'm pleased that your life has been successful and thankful that you can provide our children with so many opportunities. I hope each of them will learn from your example and lead worthwhile and fulfilling lives.

May 20

I've put off writing about us, but now I must face the task of discussing our marriage and my decision to leave you. Perhaps it is a gift I've been given—the knowledge that I am dying but with time to prepare for it. So I have this opportunity to be totally honest with you and with myself as well.

Be assured that I did love you and have only the most wonderful memories of the first years of our marriage. I also know that the sadness over the loss of our two babies took a toll on our relationship. We each tried to deal with our sadness in our separate ways instead of coming together and comforting each other. I don't know when your feelings for me changed or if they truly did change. I know my feelings for you hadn't changed, but perhaps I didn't communicate my love and need for you.

You well know that when Wilhelmina told me she was carrying your child, it was the most devastating day of my life. I felt so ill that I truly thought I might lose my own baby. I didn't think I could survive the loss of another child. I had to get away from you. I still marvel that Henry was born such a healthy, happy baby after the agony I suffered while I carried him.

I still don't understand why you sought Wilhelmina's company in place of mine. People had told me that I was a fine-looking woman at thirty, but of course, not so young as Wilhelmina. I was the mother of your four children and your partner in the business. We shared so much together during our twelve years of marriage—both great happiness and terrible sorrow when our two babies died. If only you had come to me sooner if you were unhappy in our marriage. But perhaps you thought I wouldn't understand, and I may not have accepted or understood any criticism of me. Perhaps you thought that I should just be happy with my beautiful new home, wonderful children, and prosperous husband, and accept what you might have thought was a privilege due your success. Whatever your reasons for deceiving me, my anger was too intense to listen to any apologies. I felt humiliated, and I couldn't bear to think that others might now see me as a foolish woman, shamed and forsaken by her own husband. I did not think I would ever be able to respect or trust you again or to respect myself if I accepted your deceit and stayed with you. I have always been a proud woman. That pride made it impossible for me to listen to your entreaties to forgive you and come home. They say that pride is the worst of the seven sins, so I must ask for God's forgiveness. But I cannot ask His forgiveness unless I also can forgive. I am sure that He will forgive me. I am sorry that I was unable to forgive you then.

Would it have been possible to heal our marriage if I had returned? I don't know, but I do now recognize that I also made mistakes. I was selfish, putting my anger and pride above the concern for our children. I didn't think through the effect of taking them away from a father to help raise and guide them and from a man who loved them as deeply as they loved him. I didn't think clearly about the permanence of my words. I suppose some part of me wanted to punish you, and certainly Wilhelmina also suffered the brunt of my anger. She was so young and probably terribly frightened by the situation in which she found herself. With no means of support and perhaps even the condemnation of her family and friends, I'm sure she was desperate. Now that time has passed, I certainly cannot fault you for marrying her—you did the honorable thing. I have only myself to blame for not reconciling our marriage.

May 21

I shed many tears yesterday thinking of what might have been, but then I realized how my life has been blessed by James and my little girls. So I am ready to continue . . .

When you arrived at my sister's house in Des Moines and pleaded with me to forgive you, I told you that the only thing you could do to make me happy was to give me a divorce. You gave into my demands. I regretted my words many times over the next few weeks, realizing how much the children missed you. I didn't think I could feel any more brokenhearted than I had when you first admitted your guilt, but when the divorce papers arrived, along with a letter from Mr. Stebbens telling me of your plans to marry Wilhelmina, it felt like a knife was being twisted through my heart. Poor Ruth tried to comfort me but had no answer to my constant question, "When am I going to stop making the wrong choices in my life?"

Eventually, I realized that it was too late to undo the decisions I had made, and I had to face up to my choices and make the best of the situation for the sake of our children. I had to be strong, and I had to be the best mother that I could possibly be. So I moved forward with my life. I focused every bit of my energy caring for baby Henry and the older children when they were home from school. I just wanted to provide some happiness in their lives.

I did not think I would ever be able to trust or care for any man again, but then I met James. He gave me his love so unconditionally, recognizing that I was still a shattered woman but giving me the time I needed to heal. It couldn't have been easy for him, but he was always patient. We were married within the year. His love and patience made him a wonderful stepfather and father to our three little girls. With the birth of Emily, followed by Elsie and Maria, my life finally turned around. It was again filled with love and purpose, and I know I am a better person now than the angry and bitter woman who left Davenport seven years ago.

When you come to Denver to get Henry and Louise, I hope that you will meet my beautiful little girls. Everyone tells me that Emily looks just like me—I wonder if you will think so too. Louise Lauche will continue to help me care for them, but James and I must decide what their future will be after I'm gone. James loves them so dearly but can't possibly manage three little girls by himself. How can God bring this sorrow again on such a good man? But I must not question His will. It is just so devastating to add more loss to James's life—I pray daily that God will provide the comfort and strength he needs. It is not dying that causes me such sadness but the pain my death will bring to my husband and the uncertainty of the future for my sweet babies. At least James will remember my love, and I must believe that God will take care of the rest.

I will end this letter to you so that I can write to Willie and Carl. Please come soon, and I pray for enough time left on this earth to see you once again. I thank you for blessing my life with our four wonderful children. I am so proud of each of them, and I know you are a good father who loves them, and that gives me much comfort. Before you arrive, I will write letters to Louise and Henry, which I will leave with you. Please pass them on when you think the time is right. Soon I will be reunited with our dear babies, Nonnie and Marie. I am grateful for the happiness and love that I shared with both you and James and for the time I've had with my seven children.

Don't be sad for me. Writing this letter to you has brought me much peace. Traugott, your name expresses what I now will do, "Trust in God."

Goodbye for now,
Marie

Faithfully translated for Emily Bowers Lawton

Traugott Richter, April 19, 1903

Part 3

Marie and James

Rockvale, June 24, 1904

Dear Emily,

Mama and I wish you a very happy birthday! I hope this letter finds you well and happy. Since you have now arrived at the legal age of twenty-one, it is my duty as the executor of your father's will to distribute to you the money from his estate that was divided equally between you and your two sisters and placed in trust until each of you turned twenty-one. I know there was not a significant amount left from the sale of the three homes and saloon after all the debts were paid. The Panic of 1893 and the Depression that followed severely affected the price I could get from the sale of the property owned by your parents. According to your father's instructions, I placed the money in the bank. That money has been forwarded to you now via a bank draft. I have enclosed with this letter an accounting of money and statements from the bank over the past twelve years. Included in the bank deposit box was an envelope with your name on it—James told me that he had saved some letters that must be passed on to you when you were old enough to understand and appreciate them. I am enclosing the envelope along with a certified copy of your father's will and records of the property sales. I will continue to act as executor of the remaining estate until Elsie and Maria each turn twenty-one.

Mama Davis and I loved you girls very much and hated allowing you to leave us, especially as your father had assigned us to be your guardians in his will. When Mr. Richter sent a letter with William to your father, he convinced him that it was in your best interest to live with the Richter family in Davenport. Your father realized that Traugott could provide a much better life for you girls than anything we could afford. Even more than the letter, it was probably William's presence here that finally made your father change his mind. James knew that Willie was a fine young man and trusted his judgment. When he confirmed that we should allow you to go to Davenport, James agreed. Just days before his passing, James told us of his decision. We knew it would be hard, but we had to respect James's final wishes.

We both missed you so much after you left and always looked forward to receiving your letters. It has been a while now since we have heard from you, but we understand that your life as a married woman is much busier than before. We did love hearing about your plans for the wedding in your last letter and hope that everything in your life has turned out just as you had hoped. Please let us know that this packet has arrived safely, and if you can find the time, let us know how you are getting along.

Our regards to Horace—we feel like we know him from your letters over the years, and our love to your sisters, Elsie and Maria.

> With sincerest affection,
> Papa Davis

*   *   *

July 21, 1887

Dearest James![1]

It is a beautiful summer afternoon and the time has come to write to you the letter that I've been composing in my head now for several weeks. Maria is napping and Lulu has taken Elsie and Emily outside to play and I've asked her to give me an hour by myself—and so my dear even if it seems strange I write to you rather than talk to you, but it is easier that way for me. Though my written English has many errors, it is still easier for me to find the right words to express my feelings when I have time to think about what I want to say and I know it is so hard for you to listen when I talk about my death so I think it will be best for both of us if I put my thoughts on paper. My darling, I'm quite sure now that death is not long away, and I have so much that I must say to you, someday I hope that you share this letter with our girls so that they come to know me a little better and know how much I loved you and them! Please tell them that every day after I am gone. I tell you it is the only thing that truely frightens me about death—what will happen to our girls? Not knowing that is much more frightening than any other uncertainty. God willing, I will watch over you and our girls from above.

---

[1] I have two of the letters that Marie wrote to James (see "Family History"), which served as my guide in creating this letter. I used some of her exact words and phrases, but primarily I just tried to duplicate her style. She made a few spelling errors, but most of those were simple words such as "git" for *get* and "shurley" for *surely*, and she used some incorrect verb tenses such as "sent" instead of *send*. Primarily, she used many run-on sentences, and in place of periods, she frequently used commas and dashes. She also used exclamation marks at the end of sentences, following the greeting, and after her signature.

We have talked a little about how you can care for the girls when I am gone and I know how much you also love them and want what is best for them—they are so young and they need a mother! Lulu is truly kind and has been such a help to me these past six months, but she cannot be a full time mother to our girls since she will marry her sweet John soon and they will move to their own home and start a family. My sister Ruth in Des Moines would take the girls but that would be just too far away from you—I desire that you should be as much as part of their lives as possible—they need your love now more than ever!

I know that you had no choices but to give up your infant daughter when your first wife died during childbirth and you had no way of knowing that you would be giving her up forever because her foster parents couldn't bear to part with her. It was the right thing to do for your daughter who had come to love her substitute parents as much as anyone could love their own birth parents now my dear I just don't want you to be separated forever from Emily, Elsie and Maria as they must know you and love you as their father!

It is equally important to me that the girls not be separated from each other and must grow up together—you cannot manage to run the boarding house and saloon and to raise three girls all under five years of age. Now my dear I shurley think the best choice will be to sent them to Rockvale to live with the Davis family. Maude and John are such good friends of yours and I know they would do anything to help you through this time of great need. They are good parents to their Maggie and Ella and their girls are old enough to help care for Emily, Elsie, and Maria. The Davis house is small but I think they will be able to manage with five girls.

Of course, I have had no change of mind about the hard time it is to raise a family in a coal mining town even though it has grown in the past few years and is a real town now, at least there is now a school and even a Methodist Church. More important it is to me that they are raised by a family who will love them and instill good values and they will be close to you my dear!

The rent on our houses should be enough to provide Maude and John with money to cover the daily living expenses for the girls even though they may tell you that it isn't necessary to give them money, I want you to do so as they must not experience any sacrifice to take our daughters into their home and our girls must be well cared for, don't you think the same?—You see James I am so glad now that we bought the three lots on Larimer Street and built our little house and two others to rent out! Rental property is always a safe source of income. Shurely with the money you provide they can put some aside and add a room onto their home. You see my dear husband we would not have been able to build our homes so soon if it hadn't been for the money I received from Traugott and now you can do the same for John and Maude—the money you give them each month should be enough to cover the added expenses for our girls with a little extra they can set aside to make bigger their home. Now you see, I still think about money too much, but the most important thing is your visits—you could take the Topeka and Santa Fe and get to Rockvale in just a couple hours to visit our girls as often as possible.

By the time the girls are twelve, I want that they could come back to Denver to live with you and complete their schooling here. There is a fine, big high school in Denver and none in Rockvale so they would have to travel to Florence each day so it would be much easier and better for them to get their education in Denver, and you know how important that is to me! So, my dear please keep a close eye on their schooling throughout their childhood. In mining towns many of the young boys drop out of school to work in the mines, even as young as ten years of age because their parents don't recognize the need for a good education and soon after the young girls drop out of school too. That must not happen to Emily, Elsie and Maria. James my Dear talk to them about school and make sure that they know how important it is and read to them every night just as I have always done. I think they are all very bright little girls, and I want them to grow up to be self-sufficient women.

If you were to marry again, then the girls could live with you and your new wife. I know you don't want to hear me say it but you must know my feelings about all matters. I know that you loved your first wife but that took nothing away from your love for me, and neither will a future love diminish the love I know you felt for me. I only beg of you that you find a wife who will love our girls with all her heart and be a good and kind mother for them! Now I must rest.

July 27, 1887 (Wednesday)

Some days I think it is only my desire to write to you and our girls that keeps me going as long as I have as it is important to me to leave these letters with you so that you will always be able to look back on them and be reminded of my love for you.

Do you remember the day we met when Ruth's husband Conrad invited you to dinner? I'm sure he understood our mutual need and thought that we would find comfort in each other. Being the sweet man that you are, you told me later that you fell in love with me that first day. I was not yet ready to love again, but each time we were together my respect and fondness for you grew.

From the start I recognized that you were a true gentleman as well as a gentle man. You did not at all fit my image of a saloon-keeper from a mining town out west but I loved hearing your stories about Colorado as you saw so much beauty there and your descriptions were like poetry. I could see that it would be a place where I would not feel so downhearted and I could have a happy future.

Why James you were always so kind and patient with me no matter when I am some times very queer in my ways but you understood the bad experience I had and how much falsehood I suffered through and always forgave my strange behavior and your honesty and faithfulness taught me to trust again.

Dear husband from the first time you met my children you treated them with kindness and respect—you would play ball with Willie and Carl and listened to their stories like every word they said was the most interesting thing you had ever heard and you sat on the floor and shared tea parties with little Louise, and she soon thought of you as her favorite playmate and you held baby Henry in your arms like he was your own child. I still find it hard to imagine that you wanted to marry a woman with four young children, the oldest only nine and the youngest still an infant. My good husband from the very start you have been such a good step-father to them.

I thought I could write more today, but I am so tired that I must stop again for now.

July 28, 1887 (Thursday)

You made me very happy when you asked me to marry you as I recognized my need for you and my children's need for a loving father! I trusted in your promises to always be a faithful husband because I had no doubt that you were an honorable man and I also knew we were kindred spirits when we shared our dreams of starting a new life for ourselves. We made arrangements quickly so that we could travel to Denver before the worst of the winter storms might begin and with Conrad and Ruth's blessing we said our vows in the little Lutheran Church in Indianola and packed up our family and belongings to begin our journey westward on the train. The children were excited also to begin a new adventure and see mountains for the first time and we were happy even though I must admit I was also a bit nervous. Shurley my dear you must have known some hesitations too.

When we got off the train at the magnificent new Union Station in Denver I knew that this was a place where I could live as it was a city slightly larger than Davenport, and the Tabor Opera House had just opened and promised to be even grander than the Burtis Opera House in Davenport. Of course, with the State Capitol building right there on Larimer and Eighteenth Street along with the banks, a Court House and Post Office, elegant hotels, and many brick business buildings Denver was a boom town with a bright future. They said that it was growing by one hundred people every day and it seemed like we should be part of that!

Then you took me to see Rockvale, and I could see beauty only in the distant mountains but not in the coal camp it was then. Mrs. Boyd was a sweet woman and certainly ran a clean boarding house so we had a decent place to stay there and

Maude and John welcomed me and I know they wanted for us to settle there but I could not raise my children in such a place they were accustomed to a much different way of life, and I would not subject them to such a change. Dear James did you think your new wife was altogether too high and mighty? But I also truely believed that together we could build a much more successful business with a brand new start in Denver. You always respected my opinions, wanted what was best for my children, and would do whatever it took to make me happy. So you left your friends and saloon in Rockvale, and we went back to Denver and in the end, I think that it worked out well for the Davises too managing your saloon John was able to git out of the coal mines and had a much safer and more stable job. I know most of your profits were used up in paying salaries, but I still believe we made the right decision for the good of my children don't you agree?

First we had to find a home to rent so my children would have a place to live and could get started in school and we found a comfortable little place that was close enough to the business district that we could get between home and work even when the snow was piled high though I hated paying out $12 each month in rent! Then we had to find a property for our business and I still think the little brick building we selected in Curtis Park was just the right size and location right on the street car line but perhaps too far away from the train station and big hotels. I know that you wanted to start small with just a saloon like the one you owned in Rockvale but I was concerned about the possible effect of the temperance movement and encouraged you to add sleeping quarters on the second floor as it seemed like a way to git more business with the many miners who stopped in Denver to pick up supplies on their way to Leadville but I didn't think about the kind of place most of those miners were searching for, and they were much more interested in spending their time and money in the bordellos and gambling establishments on Hollady Street. Those men who had the money and prestige frequented the finer hotels like the Windsor and the American House and saloons such as the Palace—it has been hard to compete with the upper scale establishments. My concern over prohibition of liquor has not been validated and the boarding house has made your work much harder especially now My dear I pray that you will find someone you can trust to help with the management of the boarding house so that you will have the time in your life to spend with our daughters.

Again, I will continue tomorrow, God willing.

July 29, 1887 (Friday)

You did me much good last night with your loving words and always so much help for me with the girls even with you so tired from a long day of work.

My life truly turned around with the birth of our first daughter Emily. Caring for an infant again with a loving father and husband at my side reminded me of all that made my life worthwhile and I felt such joy again in those days and that joy continued with the birth of Elsie and Maria! Our life together with our three girls and my four older ones was such a different experience for me than my early years of motherhood. Of course, Henry was born at such a low point in my life—I don't know what I would have done without Ruth's help. But it was different too when Willie, Carl and Louise were born as I was still a young woman and not as mature in my ways but there is also so much difference between you and Traugott. His focus and mine too was always on the business, and even though he loved our babies, he was not help with them the way you have helped me. Truely in spite of all I am shure he will be a good father to Willie, Carl, Louise and Henry now. Their letters to me have helped me feel confident in our decision to send them back to Davenport. For me, I am such a fortunate woman to have experienced your love—a caring man and loving father who has adored his three little girls from the day of their birth! I love to see Emily and Elsie rush to your arms when you return home from work with little Maria toddling right behind. You are a good man, my dear James, and I love you so very much!

You helped me through the most difficult times in my life when I was so sad that we sent Willie and Carl back to Davenport, and I know you missed them too. But you reminded me that our boys were almost grown and there comes a time when all parents must let go and allow their children to create their own lives and you said that it is our job to raise our children to be independent. You reminded me that I was only seventeen when I left my parents and home in Germany to come to America only now do I realize how hard that must have been for my parents to let me go and yet they knew that would be best for me. Now I have learned from you to be strong enough to do what is best for my children as I had to do when we sent Louise and Henry away—shurley it was having you at my side that gave me the strength to say good bye when Traugott came to git them! My dear James, you are so wise in understanding people and life, and sometimes I think my head was just made to understand numbers. I thank God that you came into my life and taught me so much about love and I'm grateful that Willie, Carl, Louise and Henry all had the opportunity to experience your influence in their lives.

Please my dear write to them often in Davenport so that they will always remember you and be reminded of the love that both of us had for them!

You must be strong now for our Emily, Elsie and Maria. They will need you to be there for them as much as you possibly can—guide them and love them. I know it will be hard on you but I am confident you can manage it for the sake of your love for me and our girls.

I will write now to our girls and I want you to save this letter to give to them when they are old enough to understand.

I hope that you know that no person in this world is dearer to me than you and so my dearest James, I thank you for giving me a second chance at happiness and love—both to be loved and to love. Don't be sad for me now because I have been richly blessed.

May God bless you and keep you and our girls safe and happy until we meet again where we will never be parted.

With my abiding love forever,
Marie!

*   *   *

August 2, 1887

My dear, dear girls, Emily, Elsie, and Maria!

I'm sorry that I can't write to each of you separately, but I don't think I will be granted much more time on this earth. I am dictating this letter to Lulu Lauche, our good friend and neighbor, because I no longer have the strength to write. I've told Lulu that she should make sure that my grammar is correct, but not to change a single thought. I will leave this letter with your father so that he can share it with you when the time is right.

Preacher Reed has been to visit me several times in the past few weeks and he assures me that I will soon be in a better place. I can't imagine a better place than right here on earth with the three of you and your loving father, my dear husband, James. My only prayer now is that God will grant me the chance to watch over each of you and that we will all be united again in a distant time.

Emily, what a sweet, loving, thoughtful little girl you are and such a responsible big sister too! You seem to have an innate ability to know just what your sisters need and are always truly generous and helpful. You are so caring of your little sisters, and someday you will be a wonderful mother too. I can already see what a bright girl you are. Always work hard to fulfill your potential and stay as sweet as you are. Elsie, you and Emily are so much alike. I watch you try to do everything that Emily does, to be just like her—that is good that you should follow her example. I know you will always be the best of friends. You must continue to care for each other throughout your lives and together watch over your baby sister too. Maria, what a dear, beautiful baby you are. I can already see the same sweetness in you just like your two older sisters. I love hearing your happy laugh from the time you awake each morning; I hope and pray you will always be so happy.

When I am gone, you will go to live with Maude and John Davis. They are wonderful, kind people who will take good care of you. I know that you will have a good home with them. Your father will visit you often. Even if he can't be there day by day, his love will always be with you.

I hope that someday you will be able to meet your older brothers and sister who are all living in Davenport now. They are growing up to be fine young people, and I know they also care for you. You may not remember them, but they will remember you and will always think of you with love.

Don't be sad for me. Your father has taught me, by his example, to think of others and to love again—and that has brought contentment to my life. I will share a story with you. One day last year I was out doing the shopping with the boys. We saw a poor beggar woman on the street who said she had had nothing to eat for two days. James was away on business in Rockvale, and we were running short of cash ourselves. However, Willie had made money selling newspapers and always gave everything he earned to me. I took some of that money and gave it to the woman so she could buy some bread and piece of fruit. Willie was most concerned that I would give away his hard-earned money. I tried to explain that the poor woman needed it more than us. Henry truly understood, and he reminded Willie that just as it made him happy to give his money to me, it made me happy to be able to help someone else whose need was even greater than ours. This is the lesson I have learned from your father. It is not what we get that brings us the greatest happiness but rather what we can give to others.

I wish that I could be with you longer to teach you some of the other lessons I've learned in life, but I know your father will guide you well. Be thankful for your blessings, and trust in God. Pray for His guidance and the strength you will need to handle whatever comes in your lives. You must also always try to do your best. The efforts you invest will provide satisfaction. Don't fear failure but learn from your mistakes. You cannot control everything that happens in your lives, but you can control your own response to those events. Be sure that you also make time for those things that bring you joy whether it's music or art or books or friends or enjoying the wonders of God's creation. Treat others with kindness and respect, and cherish your family.

All I can give now are my hopes for your futures. I hope your lives will be fulfilling. I hope you will find contentment and happiness. I hope you will have the strength to meet every challenge with courage and honor. I hope your lives will be blessed by love.

Your dear father and all my wonderful children have made my life complete and happy. You are the richest blessings of my life.

> With love forever, in this life and the next,
> Mama

*   *   *

Davenport, Iowa July 18, 1904

Dear Mama and Papa Davis,

Thank you so much for your kind letter and sending the money that was left to me by my papa. Thank you also for handling his estate all these years and continuing to do so for Elsie and Maria. I didn't even realize that there would be an inheritance, so it came as a pleasant surprise to receive something. But the most valuable gifts to me were the letters from my mother.

The first letter was one that my mother wrote to my papa in which she described how grateful she was for the time in her life that she shared with him. She truly believed that he had not only changed her life, but because of his love for her, she also learned to love again. He represented her second chance in life, and she loved him dearly. She also wrote a letter to Elsie, Maria, and me. She loved us so very much, and she expressed her hopes for our lives. Her letter helped me to realize that she was not afraid of death because of her faith in God and because her short life on earth had been filled with people she loved. Of course, she didn't want to leave us, but she was at peace in the end. If she is looking down on us now, I'm sure that she is happy knowing we've all had good lives. I hope I have lived up to her ideals and her hopes. I may not remember my mother, but now I feel that I truly know her, and I admire her so much.

In addition, I have been given the opportunity to learn more about my mother's life with Papa Richter. He died in the hospital following an operation last month, just after my birthday. He left me a detailed letter describing his life with my mother and his love for her, and he also translated for me a letter she wrote to him. Those two letters answered all the questions I have asked about my mother for the past twelve years. I was relieved to learn that my mother had forgiven him and they had reconciled their differences before she died.

I am thankful that I could visit Papa Richter before he died and tell him how much I loved him. He asked me to forgive him too, but I said there was nothing to forgive. I told him that he was a wonderful father to my sisters and me and nothing else mattered; I would always love him. He smiled then and said that he loved me too. Now that I've read his letter, I understand why he asked for forgiveness. I just hope that I was able to convince him that I loved him for what he was to me—a true Papa. I also understand now why we three girls were so important to him. He never stopped loving my mother, and we gave him a chance to demonstrate his love for her. I know he still knew me at the end, but when he said that he loved me, he called me "Marie."

In truth, my mother was a fortunate woman. She was greatly loved by two men in her life, and she loved both in return.

And now for the best news of all: This year has been so incredible for me because it is the beginning of a new chapter in my life—motherhood. In February, I gave birth to a healthy, happy baby boy. We named him Leslie, and he has filled my life with joy. Now that I am a mother myself, I can understand so much more about the love my mother described in her letters. I'm sure that she loved me just as much as I love my baby.

Finally, I realize that I was not really a "poor orphan" after all. The experiences that I faced growing up enriched my life. Just think of all the people who loved me—my own mother and father, the two of you, Papa Richter, my own sisters, Elsie, Maria, my Colorado sisters, and all my Davenport brothers and sisters and nieces and nephews. And now added to that list is my dear husband, Horace, and our baby Leslie. My mother said in her final letter that to love and be loved was her life's richest blessing. What a privilege it has been for me to love and be loved by so many people.

With a grateful heart and much love,
Emily

Epilogue
Emily

Davenport, August 8, 1919

Dearest Maggie,

I received your letter and was so sorry to hear about the death of Mama Davis, and it's truly hard to believe that Papa Davis passed away four years ago. I wish I had known as I certainly would have written my condolences then. They were a true mother and father to me and my sisters for five years of our young lives. After we left Colorado, it was the letters I received from them that gave me the strength to accept and adjust to my new life in Davenport. I know you and Ella will miss them so very much, as will all their grandchildren. I am glad that you were able to move back to live with Mama Davis after Papa died and care for her during her final years. It makes me feel better knowing she was always surrounded by people who loved her.

I am thankful your home was not destroyed by the terrible fire in Rockvale that you described in your letter. I have precious memories of living in that home with you, Ella, and Mama and Papa Davis. It is hard for me to imagine so many buildings destroyed. The hotel and firehouse and some of the stores your mentioned had not even been built yet when I left Rockvale twenty-seven years ago, but I do remember the town hall and the wonderful Christmases there. For you, it must seem like the town has disappeared, but buildings can be rebuilt. I thank God that there was no loss of life when so many people could have been trapped in the theater.

I can hardly believe that it has been fifteen years since we've been in touch. How does one begin to cover so many years in one letter? I will attempt to tell you a little about my life during those years. Horace and I and our two children, Leslie and Lucy, are now living in the Lawton family home at 913 Vine. Horace's sister, Mary Cunningham, inherited all the Lawton property when Mrs. Lawton died a couple years ago. Mary spends much of her time in Glenwood Springs, Colorado, now that she is retired, and she wanted us to have the biggest of the Lawton properties for our family. It is so much nicer than the duplex we lived in previously, but I was so in love that I was totally happy where we lived. Now we have three bedrooms upstairs and a lovely big living room, dining room, kitchen, and parlor. We also have three porches and a big shaded yard to enjoy on hot summer days.

The past fifteen years have brought sadness in my life too. The worst was nine years ago when my two-year-old daughter Mary died from diphtheria. She was a beautiful child with blond, curly hair and the sweetest smile. For weeks, I didn't know if I could survive such sorrow, but then I realized my two other children needed me. Little Lucy was only three years old at the time, and Leslie was six; I just had to gather the strength to go on for their sake.

I also was very sick myself several years ago. My doctor in Davenport did what he could, but I probably would have died if it hadn't been for my brothers and sisters. Elsie took Leslie and Lucy to her house and cared for them while I was sick, but I continued to get weaker and weaker. When my doctor said I was dying, Will informed the family that they just weren't going to accept the diagnosis without first getting me the best medical care available. So one day Carl and Henry came to the house with a fur coat, wrapped me up in it, and drove me to Iowa City to see the university doctors. Amazingly, with their expertise, the best innovations in modern medicine, and many prayers, I pulled through. I try to approach each day now with gratitude for life's blessings.

I know you want to hear about my sisters, Elsie and Maria—they are both living in Omaha now. I do miss them. Elsie recently moved to Omaha, and she tells us that Maria and her husband introduced her to a very nice man, Charles Dempster. We hope there will be a future to this relationship. Maria married John Barrett nine years ago, and they have an eight-year-old girl whom they also named Marie and a six-year-old boy named John after his father. So my mother's name has again been passed on to the third generation. I named our little girl Lucille Marie.

I know you remember Will from the time he came to Rockvale to take Elsie, Maria, and me back to Davenport. He decided almost twenty years ago that the fur store was not for him and built a very successful moving and storage business in Davenport. Both of his sons, Bill and Rudy, are working with him. He is so involved in the community, always doing whatever he can to help the less fortunate—we all admire him.

Perhaps you remember some of my other brothers and sisters from the letters I wrote to Mama and Papa Davis. Henry and Carl still run Papa Richter's fur store and are very prosperous. Carl has three children. Carl Jr. works at the store, Catherine is two years older than my Lucy, and James is still in grammar school. Carl's family lives in a castle-like home overlooking the downtown so it's close to the store. Henry's only child, Traugott Jr., is the same age as my Leslie, and they are best of friends. Traugott Jr. achieved quite an honor this year—he won the Iowa state spelling bee!

My older sister, Louise, has two children. Her daughter, Marie, just graduated from Vassar and is now doing further study at Columbia. My mother would have been so proud that her oldest granddaughter (and namesake) was able to get a college education. Louise's son Henry will be attending Exeter

Academy in New Hampshire in the fall. He has been an excellent student and athlete in both track and football at Davenport High School, and he plans to attend Harvard following a year in prep school. The whole family admires the accomplishments of both Marie and Henry. Louise deserves a lot of credit since she had to raise them on her own after her husband Henry died from tuberculosis seven years ago. The whole family even traveled to the Arizona Territory, hoping for a cure. As you know, my own mother died from tuberculosis in the days when Denver was known as the "world's sanitarium." By 1910, when Henry became ill, the city of Tucson, Arizona, had become one of the favored places for "lungers" to travel for the sunshine and dry desert air. Louise said that Tucson was still a small town with dirt streets, and Arizona was not yet a state back then, but St. Mary's Sanitarium was a comfortable facility designed so that each room opened onto an interior courtyard. Louise and the children stayed at a downtown hotel and could visit daily. Marie and Henry were able to enroll in school during the year they stayed in Tucson. The warm, dry air and good nutrition and care were not enough to save Henry's life. Fortunately, he provided very well for Louise and the children. She just recently remarried and lives in a lovely colonial home near Vander Veer Park. I am happy for her.

My stepmother, Wilhelmina, still lives in the house on Ninth Street where I grew up. It's just a block away so I try to go and visit with her once a week. Sometimes Lucy will go with me, but I still don't think she especially enjoys having children around. I'm afraid that some of my childhood letters may have portrayed Wilhelmina in an unfavorable light, but I hope you saw through my childish rants and did not judge her harshly. She treated me fairly and certainly no differently than her own flesh and blood, but there were times when I just wanted a mother who would put her arms around me and tell me that I was loved, the way your mother did.

Wilhelmina and Traugott's older children, Edward, Frieda, and Alma, are all married and still living in Davenport. Edward and Frieda both have two children, and Edward manages the fur department at the store. Herbert joined the army, and after fighting in France, he came home to live in the Ninth Street house with his mother. Trudy is also living there now since she started teaching business classes at Davenport High School. The house must seem quite big and lonely with only three people and the maid living there. Just think, at one time it held fourteen people. It really was a happy home for me most of the time. Wilhelmina talks about moving to one of the elegant apartment buildings north of the high school. I know she will get something big enough for Herbert and Trudy to stay with her if they want.

Like you, I am so relieved that the terrible Great War is finally over. I am grateful that it ended before my Leslie was old enough to be called to serve. I'm also happy that Herbert is safely home. For eleven months I had been so worried about him. He was more than a little brother to me since I helped care for him from the time he was an infant. It brought to mind those terrible months back in 1898 when we all worried so about Henry. There are many families here that have lost sons, and my heart breaks for them. Almost two hundred young men from the Tri-Cities were killed.

It was unbelievable to me that in Davenport there were some German immigrants who wanted Germany to win the war. The father of one of Lucy's playmates was one of them. He owns a very successful company and lives in a lovely home, and yet in spite of the life he established here, he backed Germany. It's not that he opposed America, but rather he wanted America to stay out of the conflict with the hope that Germany would be able to establish an empire in Europe. I don't understand that. Immigrants came here to build a better life for themselves and their families, and many of them succeeded in fulfilling their dreams. Their allegiance now should be to America. I'm glad that Papa Richter was proud to be an American citizen, and he instilled that pride in all his children too. He knew that America truly was his land of opportunity, and he appreciated that he was able to work hard and provide a wonderful life for his family.

But there are two sides to every issue, and there were unfortunate occurrences in Davenport in some of the German neighborhoods. Innocent people were called "Kaiser Lovers" just because they were of German heritage, and some even had their front doors painted yellow in the middle of the night and their homes vandalized. Some businesses were boycotted too, but fortunately, the Richter family was always treated respectfully and the fur store continued doing a good business. I wish that people of all nationalities, religions, and races would recognize their commonalities and treat each other with respect. I don't understand why some Americans would behave with such animosity toward their neighbors. The Bible tells us to "love your neighbor as yourself," and Papa Richter always taught all of us to live by the Golden Rule. In fact, if we got into fights or were mean to one another, we had to write it one hundred times. Some of my brothers developed very good penmanship!

During the war I tried to do my part by buying war bonds and knitting scarves for our soldiers. We had a victory garden too. We grew tomatoes, lettuce, beans, and rhubarb. We have currant bushes and grapevines and planted an apple and a cherry tree. My whole family loves my grape and currant jams and rhubarb pies. I was pleased that Horace went to work at the Rock Island Arsenal. They produced so many goods needed by our fighting men, from harnesses and saddles to rifles and canteens. On the day of the Armistice, over ten thousand Arsenal employees, including Horace, were let out of work to parade through the downtowns of Davenport and Rock Island. Petersen's Department Store hung an American flag from the fifth floor that almost reached to the ground. What an inspiring sight! I am holding on to my hope that this was the war to end all wars.

Our family was very fortunate not to be hit by the influenza epidemic after the war. Most public places in Davenport were closed, and there was a city-wide quarantine. Despite that, our hospitals were filled, and they had to open up a temporary hospital at the Turner Hall. The newspapers reported that over two thousand people died in the Tri-Cities—that's ten times the number killed in the war. Did the epidemic hit Rockvale hard?

I'll move on to a happier topic, my children. Leslie is at Davenport High School. He loves to read and always has his head buried in a book in the evening. He would certainly rather read than do his homework. He is struggling a bit with Latin, but I enjoy working with him. Perhaps because I didn't get the opportunity to become a teacher myself, I love helping my children with their homework. I enjoy the challenge of remembering things I learned long ago and learning other skills for the first time right along with them.

Lucy is in intermediate school now. She was disappointed when she learned that she wouldn't be attending the same school as her best friend, but she has adjusted and made new friends. Lucy is doing fine in school and excels in math. She must have inherited that ability from my mother. She is relieved that she no longer is required to study German in school. Before the war, she had told her teacher that she wanted to drop her German class, but the teacher said that she would never be able to get a job if she couldn't speak German. Once the United States became involved in the war, all German language classes were dropped from the curriculum; even some German books were burned and the German newspapers went out of business.

Leslie certainly did inherit his father's talent at baseball. He loves it just as much as Horace, and the two of them are always practicing in the backyard or in the pasture only a block away from our house. Leslie also plays on the high school basketball team and takes gymnastics at the Turners. He enjoys all sports and excels at many. Lucy is very musical—just like Horace. She plays the piano well and loves to sing along with Horace while he plays his banjo. Horace gets so much enjoyment from that because Leslie and I can't carry a tune.

I was happy that the Nineteenth Amendment has finally passed both the House and the Senate. I know that women have had the privilege of voting in Colorado and many western states for a long time, but it is time for every woman in our country to be allowed to vote. It will certainly soon be ratified in all the states—it is long overdue. I have told Lucy that she must never take for granted the opportunity to vote because many women fought long and hard to gain that privilege for the rest of us.

I have rambled on long enough, but it was good to hear from you after all these years. I feel so guilty that I lost touch with Mama and Papa Davis, and now it is too late to remedy that. I'm grateful that they lived long lives filled with the love of their family. Please express my sympathy and love to Ella and to all your children and grandchildren. I surely hope that some-day I will be able to travel back to Colorado. It would be so thrilling to see all of you again and to meet your husbands and children. I wonder if I would recognize anything in Rockvale or Denver—I'm sure it all has changed so much. In the meantime,

I will write to Elsie and Maria, and I'm sure that they will both write to you too.

As my own mother said and I truly believe, the love that we share with our family and friends is life's richest blessing.

With love,
Your "sister" and friend,
Emily

Family History

Notes from the Author

Historical fiction has always been my favorite genre, in literature, television, and movies. I especially enjoyed books related to places I've lived or traveled as well as times and places in which my family had lived. Since this story was first written for my family to relate information about our ancestors, I want to specify what is factual and what was generated by stories that were told to me.

When my mother first told me stories about Emily, Marie, and Traugott, I thought it could be the basis of a good love story, and my mother thought I should write it. In addition, their lives provided lessons in dealing with adversity and examples of the strength, determination, and independence of women despite both laws and mores that discriminated against them during that time in history. The idea of writing a book remained in the back of my mind for fifty years. With the time afforded by retirement and the motivation provided by the birth of my grandchildren, I decided to finally write the story about the lives of my grandmother and great-grandmother.

I regret never having asked my grandmother about her experiences and feelings as she was growing up and therefore can only retell a few of those that were handed down by my mother. What an opportunity I missed! The numerous gaps in the stories I had heard were filled in with details related to the time periods in Denver, Rockvale, and Davenport as well as many stories that were solely imaginative.

I changed some facts concerning the family to make it less complicated, decreasing the number of siblings from fifteen to twelve and changing some names that I thought might be confusing. Marie had two daughters named Louise (Louise

Richter and Louise Bowers). The Elsie in this book is a composite of two people, the real Elsie Richter, born May 20, 1880, when Marie was in Des Moines, and Louise Bowers, my grandmother's younger sister, who was born in 1884. Herbie is also a composite of two brothers, Herbert and Traugott. I changed some dates of birth to aid in creating stories that concerned the relationships between the characters. Henry was really born in 1878, but I chose to make him closer in age to Emily. Two girls born to Traugott and Marie died soon after their births: one was their first child born in 1870, and the other was born in 1877, not consecutively as in my story. They had five children who lived to adulthood: William, Carl, Louise, Henry, and Elsie. James and Marie had three girls: Emily, Louise, and Marie. Traugott and Wilhelmina had seven children, two of whom (August and Traugott) were not included in my book. There was one Traugott and one Marie in the second generation and several more with those names in the third generation of descendants.

There is no record that Emily kept in touch with the Davis family in Rockvale during her childhood. There is one letter that she received from Maggie Davis (Mrs. W. K. Jones) in 1917 that was written in response to a letter that Emily wrote to Maggie's mother. It appears in the biographical section that follows.

Much of part 1 comes from imagining what Emily's childhood might have been. Will Richter did go to Rockvale to bring the three sisters back to Davenport to live with the Richter family. Each older child was assigned the care of one of the younger children—probably a common practice in large families. Although it seems that Wilhelmina was not close to her stepchildren, there was nothing in the stories I heard to indicate she was ever unkind to them. Horace was an orphan train child who was adopted by the Lawton family, and many of the stories about him were told to me by my mother. I don't know when Emily first met Horace, but they did live in the same neighborhood. Emily went to public school, and Horace attended parochial schools; Horace was three years older than Emily.

I have some of the memorabilia that was mentioned in Emily's letters, including furniture, china, the patchwork quilt made by Mary Lawton Cunningham in 1884, Horace's scrapbook, and the Kuhnen Medal that my grandmother received in 1896 for "academic excellence, attendance, and deportment." I also have Emily's autograph album from Rockvale, Colorado, dated April 7, 1892, which was given to her by William Richter. He autographed the book:

"to Emily—With best and kindest wishes,
From your brother—Willie."

It was the date on the album that indicates William was in Rockvale before James died on April 17, 1892. I have the last will and testament of James Bowers, dated March 22, 1892, which appoints John M. Davis as guardian of the children. Therefore, it is logical to assume that Will Richter must have influenced James to change his mind about the guardianship when he came to Rockvale in April of that year, just before James died. Emily's autograph book contains messages from friends and teachers as well as the following written on April 22, 1892:

"don't forget Mama and Papa Davis"

Since I grew up in Davenport in the 1950s, many of the locations I used in part 1 of the story were familiar to me. My grandmother and uncle lived in the Lawton home on Vine Street until her death in 1961. I lived next door, and both yards had large gardens and fruit trees. We always had tomatoes, beans, lettuce, rhubarb, currants, grapes, apples, and cherries. My mother and grandmother did a lot of canning, and Mom made fabulous pies. During my childhood, I played in the neighborhood of the Ninth Street Richter home, which had been demolished by that time. Marie's Castle was (and is) still standing. I rode my bike north on Marquette Street to Duck Creek and loved exploring the banks and wooded ravines where my Uncle Les swam in his boyhood days. Credit Island (Suburban Park) and Vander Veer (Central Park) were my favorite places to ice skate in the winter. Many of my childhood activities centered around St. Mark's Lutheran Church in west Davenport, Jefferson School (across the street from Marie's Castle), and later J. B. Young Junior High and Davenport Central High School.

Part 2 is loosely based on the stories my mother told about Marie and Traugott, along with information about Traugott from his obituary. The stories about how they met are fiction. The Richter store was started by Traugott, and Marie helped him run the business. In 1880, Marie left him after their maid, Wilhelmina, told her that she was pregnant with Traugott's child. I have no idea of circumstances that might have led up to the affair. At that time, Marie was also expecting a baby, and she took her children and went to her sister's home in Des Moines. Traugott went to Des Moines and pleaded with her to return, but she refused. After their divorce in 1880, Traugott married Wilhelmina, and again, I don't know anything about the relationship between Traugott and Wilhelmina during their marriage. In 1881, Marie married James Bowers. I was told that William and Carl went back to Davenport to work with their father in the store and learn the business. The information I discovered in researching this book seems to indicate that they were still living with Marie and James the year of her death. Attributing Marie's death to tuberculosis was my invention to provide the time needed for her to write letters, which are primarily fiction.

Other than a photo of James Bowers, I know very little about my biological great-grandfather. I was told that he was a widower, and his baby girl was raised by friends after his first wife died. Marie's two notes to him seem to indicate a loving relationship between the two of them and with all the children. These letters also indicate that Marie still harbored hurt or bitter feelings toward Traugott by her reference to a "bad experience" and to living with "much falsehood." Part 3 is based on these two notes and one additional letter, which are reproduced in the biographical information that follows. There are many mistakes in Marie's spelling and grammar, which I tried to emulate in her letter to James. Her penmanship was beautiful.

In one of Marie's letters to James, she writes about buying two lots on Larimer Street with money she was expecting in the mail. And she seems to expect James to reimburse her! In James's will, written shortly before his death, he refers to maintenance of his children coming from the rent on buildings in Rockvale, Colorado, consisting of "one lot and storeroom with dwelling, one lot and saloon building recorded in the County Clerk's office in the name Mrs. Marie Bowers." There is obviously an inconsistency in the location of his properties that I cannot explain. According to the stories I heard, he had either an inn or a saloon in Denver, and Marie helped with the business. Perhaps he sold the Denver property at some time after her death and went to Rockvale to live.

Much of the information in the epilogue is based on stories my mother told me about her childhood. Information concerning her cousins comes from her stories as well as newspaper articles she saved.

I used many sources for research concerning the times, events, and locations in the book. Other than the Christmas story, all information about Rockvale came from Internet websites. *Davenport: A Pictorial History* by Marlys Svendsen was a major source of information on the history of Davenport. I added that information into many of Emily's letters. I obtained some additional family information from Ancestry.com, where I also connected with another descendant of Traugott and Marie, the great-great-granddaughter of Louise Richter Dunker. I contacted my second cousin to determine if she had any additional information about our ancestors. She remembered her grandfather and his brothers speaking German when they visited. She also referred to the family as "secretive" and joked about the repeated use of the same names. Only two of Wilhelmina and Traugott's children were living and still resided in Davenport during my childhood. I could learn a little about some of the others and their descendants from one letter and from obituaries I found in my mother's files and on the Internet. While visiting Davenport, I used the resources of the Davenport School Museum, the German American Heritage Center, and the genealogy department at the Davenport Public Library. The staff in each of these places was very helpful in locating information that pertained to the Richter family and history of Davenport, and that information was also incorporated into this story.

Letters, documents, excerpts from newspaper articles and books, and photos that pertain to the people in this book are included with the biographical information section that follows. My mother kept many of these things, and she also started a family tree by writing to her cousins to obtain names of descendants and dates of births and deaths. All this information was helpful in writing my book, but the first and primary inspiration was the stories she told me, which are labeled "Oral History."

However, these stories are not truly an oral history because they were not firsthand accounts and were not formally recorded or written down at the time they were told. They reflect my recollection of the stories, which in turn reflect my mother's recollection of her mother's stories. In addition, memories are affected by personal feelings and points of view. In doing the research for this book, I also discovered a few discrepancies between the stories and some of the recorded information.

Throughout her life, my grandmother remained close to many of her siblings, including those who were the children of Traugott and Wilhelmina. She considered all of them her sisters and brothers. Apparently, they got along well as children, and those still living in the area remained close as adults. My mother communicated regularly with some of her cousins or their wives and often saved their cards and letters to her. There are many members of this extended family that I never met, but I admire the things I've learned in the letters written to my mother as well as information I gathered during my research.

My mother moved away from Davenport in 2003 when she was ninety-five years of age. She was the last of the family descendants to reside there. Based on a 1979 legal record of the Rudolph M. Richter Estate, the only Richter children who had any descendants still living were Carl, Louise, Henry, Elsie, Edward, and August. Only Emily had descendants still living on the Bowers side of the family, so my immediate family represents the only living descendants of Marie and James Bowers or of the Lawton family.

I wrote this book to share my family story with my grandchildren. I hope other readers will also find it interesting.

Following is the biographical information that was available to me and was used in writing this book:

Marie Schmidt Richter Bowers (1850–1887)

Born: May 6, 1850 in Berlin, Germany[2]

Married: Traugott Richter in Henry County, IL, on Nov. 7, 1867

Moved to Davenport, Iowa, in 1868

Children: Nonnie (1870)

William (1871–1938)

Carl (1874–1947)

Louise (1875–1946)

Marie (1877)

Henry (1878–1963)

Elsie (1880–1962)

Divorced: 1880

Married: James Bowers in Indianola, Iowa, on Nov. 24, 1881; Moved to Denver, Colorado

Children: Emily (1883–1961)

Louise (1884–1964)

Marie (1866–1947)

Died: August 27, 1887; buried in Riverside Cemetery in Denver

---

[2] There are many Marie(a) Schmidts listed on Ancestry.com. One Maria Schmidt (German) came from Liverpool, arriving on May 20, 1867, at the age of seventeen. She was traveling with "Elizth" Schmidt, who was twenty-three. Another Maria Schmidt (age twenty) arrived on September 13, 1867, from Hamburg and was traveling alone. Since one source gave Marie's birthdate as 1848 instead of 1850, it is possible that she could have been one of these people. Ship records show that Marie and Traugott traveled to Germany with Will, Carl, and Louise in the mid-1870s.

Oral History: Marie was born Marie Emily Schmidt in Berlin, Germany, in 1850. She married Traugott Richter, moved to Davenport, Iowa, where Traugott opened a fur store, worked at the store and managed the business. In addition to furs, they sold clothing and Singer Sewing Machines. Traugott built an elegant Italianate mansion on Marquette Street in 1879, which he called Marie's Castle. During the years from 1870 to 1880, Marie gave birth to seven children, two of whom died in infancy—at one and three months of age.

Marie left Traugott in 1880 when she was thirty years old and pregnant with her seventh child after their maid, Wilhelmina, told her that she was also expecting a baby and Traugott was the father. Marie went to Des Moines, Iowa, to stay with her sister. She kept the girls and Henry with her, but sometime later, Carl and William went back to Davenport to live with their father so they could learn the business.[3] Traugott went to Des Moines and begged her to come back. She refused, but later it was reported she expressed the wish that she could stop making so many mistakes in her life.

Marie married James Bowers at the age of thirty-one and went to Denver, Colorado, where she used her money to buy property and helped James run a saloon or inn. She gave birth to three girls— my grandmother, Emily, and two younger girls, Louise (Lulu) and Marie. She died at the age of thirty-seven, perhaps of appendicitis. Traugott went to Denver after her death and took his children back to Davenport. The three girls from her marriage to James went to live with the John Davis

---

[3]   There is conflicting information in the letters. Will was in Denver with Marie when she wrote a letter to James on February 11, 1887. Another letter based on information from Marie's neighbor states that Marie "grieved when she sent Willie and the others to Davenport." Perhaps all of Traugott's children left Denver sometime before her death in August of 1887.

family in Rockvale, Colorado. They lived there almost five years until their father's death in 1892. James remained in Denver during this time and visited his girls whenever possible. In his will written in March of 1892, he appointed John Davis as executor and guardian of his children. However, shortly before James's death, Will Richter came to Rockvale and brought my grandmother and her sisters to Davenport where they lived in the Ninth Street home with Traugott and Wilhelmina, the five half brothers and sisters who were the children of Traugott and Marie, and six children from Traugott's marriage to Wilhelmina. A seventh child was born several years later—bringing the total number of children to fifteen.

Family files contained three letters that provided some additional insight into Marie's life with James as well as a pattern I followed for the fictional letter written by Marie to James.

Marie's letter written January 26, 1887, from Denver:

My dear James!

All the children wanted to write to you and sent their best wishes to your birthday and I did make them the pleasure to sent to you a little Card for each one and you should have seen them how eager they looked in deep earnest about it thinking how happy you must feel now after this! And so my dear I sent my best wishes too: that you may live 25 years from now on anyhow and that in future we can be together and never be parted not in life nor in death! My dear I hope that you know that no person in this world is dearer to me than you, no matter when I am sometimes be very queer in my ways but think of the bad experience I had and how much falsehood I had to live with so far and you shurley will forgive me! Now my dear, Mr. Sternberg went to New York, Cleaveland and Chicago and Davenport and will not be back before 3 weeks and now good bye! and write soon, we are all well

Yours forever
Marie!

Marie's letter written February 11, 1887 from Denver:

My dear James!

I received your kind and loving letter yesterday and the children are ever so proud of the nice cards you sent them! now my dear I had not a letter yet from Davenport from Mr Carl and yesterday I received a Telegram from him telling me that he had sent letter with the enclosure of a Note Blank for more than a week ago, and that the letter must lay in the Post-office in Denver so I went there and saw Postmaster Mr Speen and I told him all about it showing him the Telegram too! He was very kind and looked the whole matter up, but could not find the letter nowhere, Mr Carl told me the same time in his Dispatch that he had mailed another letter with blank to my address, and I think I will git that to morrow now my dear I will buy than the 2 lots on Larimer Street and you my good husband see that in about 3 months can pay me the Money, you see my dear, we could build soon than and don't need to let the lots lay idle, and save the $12 rent monthly; I really think those lots are better as Mrs. Deyanes Property on Hollyday Street don't you think the same?—Why James you spoke so good and kind to me in your last letter that I hope yet I will be happy in future—Willie said last night to me, Oh mamma shall I sent papa a funny Valentine? I said no but a good and nice one you may sent and so he will, James my Dear, please sent me Money as soon as you can, I tell you I gave some Money to a poor woman what was in great need of it and so I used the Money Willie gave me this week all up already! Now my dear I feel pretty good and not so downhearted anymore, Your letter did me much good!

Now good bye
My good Husband
Yours forever
Marie!

An excerpt from Marie Barrett's letter written in 1948:

This letter provides some additional information about Marie and James Bowers and their home in Denver.

Dear Lucille,

Three weeks ago last Tuesday night Mrs. Allen and I left Omaha for a vacation in Denver where we stayed with her sister-in-law . . .

I learned a little about our family unexpectedly. Mrs. Allen's sister-in-law, Mrs. Leana Biddick, knew my grandmother Marie Bowers. In fact she knew Aunt Emily, Lulu, and mom. Her sister Mrs. Lulu Allen, nee Louise Lauche, took care of the children and Mrs. Bowers when she died. Miss Lauche was 22 then and is now 83. I talked to her and she showed me a book grandmother gave her with a note in German to her. She said that grandmother would have given her a complete works of Shakespeare if she had wanted them. She had nothing but praise of our grandmother. It was so thrilling.

One afternoon we went to Riverside Cemetery and found grandmother's grave and grandfathers. (The dates on the gravestones: James Bowers, March 11, 1845 and April 17, 1892 and Maria Bowers, May 6, 1850 and Aug. 27, 1887.)

Mr. Frantz Lauche, the father of Leana and Louise, was in business with our grandmother in Des Moines about 1875. They say our grandmother was the business brains of the business.

Mr. Lauche was a furrier. Leana and Louise lived in Davenport when small and visited later and knew the Richter side of the family. Louise said that grandmother loved her children dearly and grieved when she sent Willie and the others back to Davenport but felt they would get a better start in business from their father. Louise surely was happy to tell me all these things and her memory is very good for one 83. She lives alone in a little brick house and keeps it up herself. She lived across from the three little houses grandmother built when she was living. I do wish Aunt Emily could have talked to her as she asked me about the Richters and I couldn't tell her much. If you have any questions maybe I can find out the answers . . .[4]

Lovingly,
Marie

---

[4] Some of the information in this letter coincides with known dates. If Miss Lauche was eighty-three in 1948, then she would have been twenty-two in 1887—which was the year Marie died. However, in 1875, Marie would have been living and working in Davenport; she only lived in Des Moines from 1880 to 1881. Since Miss Lauche would have been ten years old in 1875, she may have been confused about the location or the date. Since she mentioned knowing the Richter family, it is most likely that she was referring to Davenport.

In the Denver City Directory for 1887, a Frank Lauche, furrier, was listed living at 2537 Holladay (today named Walnut St.) in Denver. This is one block from Larimer, so it is possible that Marie and James lived near Larimer and Twenty-Fifth Streets in an area known as Curtis Park. This letter refers to three houses, but Marie's own letter writes of buying only two lots.

The Curtis Park area was developed in the 1860's and contained a variety of homes from small single- story homes to row houses to large Queen Anne's. The population was diverse—ranging from prominent citizens to new immigrants of varied economic status. Denver's first streetcar line was constructed in 1871 from Seventh and Larimer to Twenty-Seventh and Champa. Many businesses and homes were built along the route.

Traugott Richter
(1844–1904)

Traugott Richter.

Born: Berlin, Germany in 1844

Married: Marie Schmidt in 1867

Children: See Marie Schmidt Richter Bowers

Died: Davenport, Iowa, in 1904; buried at Fairmount Cemetery in west Davenport

Oral History: Traugott was wearing a fur hat, which someone offered to buy from him. He sold it and then made another—thus beginning his fur business. The following articles indicate he was highly trained in Germany as a furrier and saved his money to get a start in the United States.

Divorced: 1880

Married: Wilhelmina (1858–1941) in 1880

Children: Edward (1880–1929), Elfrida (1883–1961), August (1885–1980), Alma (1886–1977), Traugott (1888–1929), Herbert (1891–1940), and Gertrude (1895–1969)

Oral History: When James Bowers died in 1892, Traugott sent his oldest son, Will, to Colorado to bring the three Bowers girls back to his home to raise them along with his own children.

Traugott's Obituary from *The Daily Times*, June 21, 1904:

PASSES AWAY AT HOSPITAL
TRAUGOTT RICHTER DIED EARLY SUNDAY MORNING
Was One of Davenport's Leading Merchants, Having
Been in Business Here Nearly Forty Years

Traugott Richter, for years one of the most prominent men in local business circles and president of the largest fur house in the west, breathed his last at Mercy hospital, Sunday morning, about 3 o'clock, after a long illness, necessitating an operation, from which he never fully recovered.

Mr. Richter was well known and generally respected in this city where he has been the leading furrier for the last 37 years. He was sixty years of age and was born in Germany May 9, 1844. Up to the time when he was 20 years of age he lived in that country, learning the fur business. At that time he emigrated to New York City and went to work at his trade in a New York establishment, resigning his position at the end of six months however to come to Dixon, Ill. where he worked in a carriage shop for a short time.

By saving every penny he amassed a small sum and with this purchased a few furs and went into business in Geneseo, Ill. In a few years by thrifty business habits and straightforward dealing with his customers he had more than trebled his original capital and he removed to Davenport and established the business on West Second Street, which he has continued in a very prosperous manner since that time.

Mr. Richter was recognized in the east as one of the best posted men on all matters pertaining to the fur business in the country. When only 19 years of age he had achieved the honor of making furs for a number of the crowned heads of Europe and their royal families and was generally known as one of the finest furriers in the country. His business in this city was built up year by year from a small establishment which he started in 1867 to the present firm of T. Richter & Sons, known as the largest fur house in the west. Two years ago Mr. Richter incorporated the business, taking in his three sons, Henry, Carl, and Edward and since that time the house has been known as T. Richter & Sons.

The survivors are Wilhelmina Richter, his wife, and twelve children, William, Carl, Henry, Mrs. Louise Dunker, Mrs. Elsie Oman of Chicago, Edward, Mrs. Freda Schwarnweber, August, Alma, Traugott Jr., Herbert, and Wilhelmina.[5] The funeral will take place Tuesday afternoon, from the home of the deceased, 1025 West Ninth Street with interment in Fairmont cemetery.

---

[5] The youngest child was Gertrude, not Wilhelmina, and in my records, Frieda's husband was Sam Banta. Perhaps that was a second marriage.

The following information about Traugott was recorded in *Historical Sketches of Prominent Men, Davenport, Iowa* in an article about Carl Richter Sr.:

> Traugott Richter, b. in Berlin, Germany, May 9, 1844. His parents, Henry and Caroline (Wolf) Richter, were native of Prussia. In 1865 Traugott Richter emigrated to America, settling in Geneseo, Ill, where he engaged in the fur business until 1868. He then established the T. Richter Fur Company, in Davenport, Iowa, and in 1902, the business became known as Traugott Richter & Company. The firm later was incorporated as T. Richter's Sons, of which Traugott Richter served as pres. the reminder of his life. He died in Davenport, June 21, 1904. He was a pioneer in Davenport and his efforts with those of the early settlers helped lay a real foundation for this community. He was interested in nearly all civic affairs of those early days and was of Lutheran faith. In 1866, he married Marie Emily Schmidt, who was b. in Berlin, Germany, May 6, 1848. She died in Denver, Colo., Aug. 5, 1887.[6] They were parents of 5 children.

---

[6] These dates regarding Marie's birth, marriage, and death differ from other sources.

James Bowers
(1845–1892)

James Bowers
1882

Born: March 11, 1845, in England

Married: Marie Richter, November 24, 1881, in Indianola, Iowa

Children:

      Emily (1883–1961)

      Louise (1884–1964)

      Marie (1886–1947)

Died: April 17, 1892, in Rockvale, Colorado; buried next to Marie in Riverside Cemetery in Denver

Oral History: James had a child by his first wife who was raised by family friends after her death—perhaps in South Dakota. When he married Marie, he asked for his child to return to live with them, but the family who was raising her pleaded with him not to take her away from them. He didn't. The 1880 Census shows James Bowers, a widower, living in Des Moines. His occupation is listed as bartender, and his place of birth is listed as England.

James Bowers's Last Will and Testament: Written on March 22, 1892: Excerpts:

> To my children Emmily Bowers, Lulu Bowers, and Marie Bowers, I give and bequeath all my personally property after my debts are paid, to Emmily Bowers, one third, to Lula Bowers one third, and one third to Marie Bowers to be paid to them as they shall arrive at the age of twenty one years.

He then goes on to list his personal property, which included a $2,000 policy, a bank deposit of $805, and a check for $540. He also mentions money that was borrowed from him from four different people and "saloon fixtures and stock in trade." It continues:

> And I hereby appoint John M. Davis my executor and guardian for my children. And I hereby authorize him to sell or otherwise dispose of my personally property as to him shall seem best and place the proceed in some good reliable Bank to the credit of my afore-mentioned children.
>
> The pay for the maintainance of anf for said children shall come from the rent of the buildings in Rockvale Colorado, consisting of one lot and store room with dwelling, one lot and saloon building recorded in the County Clerk's office in the name of Mrs. Marie Bowers.

A third page is certification from the county judge of Fremont County, Colorado, that "this is a true, correct and complete copy of the Will of James Bowers as appears from the record and files of this court. —signed March 21, 1902." [7]

---

[7] There are a lot of misspellings in this will. Assuming that James would know how to spell the names of his children, they might be typos or mistakes made by the person writing the will.

This will specifically states that the property he owns is in Rockvale, rather than in Denver, as I was told. Also, it's interesting that the property was recorded in Marie's name. Perhaps he sold the property that Marie bought in Denver (see her letter dated February 11, 1887) sometime after her death, purchased the Rockvale property, and moved there prior to the last year of his life.

Children of Traugott and Marie

William (1871–1938)

William Richter

Married: Blondina Martens (1873–1955)
Children:

William (1897–1965)

Rudolph (1900–1977)

Neither married; both went into business with their father at Ewert and Richter.

Oral History: Will (Willie), the oldest son of Traugott and Marie, came to Denver to take my grandmother and her sisters to Davenport. After some time working with his father, he decided to become a partner in a storage and transfer company, Ewert and Richter. He lived at 20 McClellen Boulevard. My mother worked for him as a secretary/bookkeeper from 1928 to 1944. She often talked about her uncle Will with love and pride.

Will Richter's Obituary from the front page of *The Daily Times*, Friday, June 24, 1938; Excerpt:

William Richter, Well Known Transfer Executive, Dies After Year's Illness at Home Today

A quiet, sincere man whose outstanding characteristics were his devotion to his business and a willingness to engage in civic and philanthropic undertakings. Mr. Richter represented one of the highest types of American citizenship. He was always deeply interested in the welfare of others less fortunately situated then himself, and one of his greatest concerns was to help improve the lot of the underprivileged. . . . He was an active member of the Chamber of Commerce and served as its president in 1923 . . . He was born in Davenport June 12, 1871, his parents, Mr. and Mrs. Traugott Richter, having come here originally from Germany. The elder Richter was in the wholesale fur business, the survivors of which are T. Richter's Sons, clothing and wholesale furs, now located at 219 West Second Street. . . . The son William lived in Davenport for the first seven years of his life,... he was 17 when he returned to Davenport and entered Duncan's Business college, following which he went into the fur business with his father. During this period he watched with interest the growth of the transfer business, and decided that it appealed to him more than furs. In the summer of 1902 he went to Herman Ewert, then conducting a successful transfer business, and broached the subject of a partnership. . . . His interest in art led him to accept a trusteeship on the board of the Municipal Art gallery. . . . Mr. Richter was of the Episcopal faith, and active in Trinity parish, being a vestryman of the cathedral for many years.[8]

From another newspaper article, it says:

With the death of William Richter, Davenport mourns a member of a pioneer family of this community who during an active business career found the opportunity to make an unselfish contribution to many phases of the life of the city. . . . Bill Richter . . . was possessed of a robust good nature, mingled with what appeared to be an exceptional regard for the sensibilities of others. He will be mourned as the type of citizen which has placed a definite stamp upon the character and culture of this city.

---

[8] Dates and locations concerning his childhood differ from the stories I was told. The obituary does indicate the Richter children lived with Marie and James until Marie's death (when Will was seventeen).

An editorial stated:

> Those who knew Will Richter best will remember him . . . for the smiling courage with which he bore the months of suffering and discouragement that preceded his death. There is an attitude of mind which is the essence of patience and courage and optimism, and this attitude Will Richter displayed thru the long months that ended with his untimely death Friday.

Carl (1874–1947)

President of T. Richter and Sons following Traugott's death.

Married: Jenny Kuhr, October 14, 1897
Children:
Carl Jr. (1898–1952), vice president of T. Richter & Sons
Married Florence McCleary
One daughter

Catherine (1904–1991)
Married: Steven Adsit
Two children

James (1908–1973)
Married: Elizabeth Summers
One daughter

A quote from the book *Davenport*, regarding an automobile parade in 1908 when there were only two hundred automobile owners in Davenport:

> The most unusual entry was that of Carl Richter. Each of Richter's passengers was

dressed in furs from head to toe—excellent advertising for the Richter Fur Company!

Carl Sr. and his family lived in a 1909 home built by Henry Struck on Sixth and Ripley Streets overlooking downtown Davenport, as pictured in the "Walking Tour Brochure" of The Gold Coast-Hamburg Historic District Association.

615 Ripley Street, "The Castle"

Excerpt from "Historical Sketches of Prominent Men, Davenport, IA":

> Mr. Richter formerly was a dir. of the First National Bank, and of the Union Savings Bank, and was a governor of the Am. Fur Assn. He is now serving as a trustee of the T. Richter Estate. He is a Republican, and a mem. of the following: Elks Lodge; Rotary Club (a charter mem.); Davenport C. of C. (a charter mem.); Davenport Turner Soc.; Davenport Country Club; and Davenport Chapter, Citizens Hist. Assn.

Louise (1875–1946)

Louise Richter
Dunker Mason

Married: Henry Dunker (1872–1912); Henry died in Arizona of tuberculosis

Married: Charles Mason, 1915

Children:

Marie Dunker Betty (1896–1959): Graduate of Vassar; postgraduate work at Smith and Columbia;

Married: H. Betty; taught at Davenport High and St. Katharine's School

Henry Dunker (1903–1975): After attending high school in Davenport, Henry went to Exeter Academy and then graduated from Harvard.

Married: Elizabeth Dennison; three children; divorced
Married: Betty Moyinhan; two children

Quote from Davenport newspaper:

> Called the greatest scholar-athlete by the *Boston Evening Transcript* as he graduated from Harvard summa cum laude. The lowest grade the school's track captain earned was one B+.

Louise Mason's home at 2018 Main Street

Henry (1878–1963)

Henry Richter

President of T. Richter Furs in 1953 when it was sold
to Rhomberg's Furs. He lived at 2513 Ripley Street

When Henry was a student in the Davenport schools, he wrote an essay about bobsledding titled "Down Gaines," stating the sled could go all the way to the middle of the river. This essay is in the Davenport School Museum with many other essays that were displayed at the Chicago Columbian Exposition in 1893. I used some ideas from his essay in my story.

Married: Minnie Stender (1880–1958)

Henry Richter's Obituary excerpt:

> When 15 Mr. Richter entered the fur business his parents founded in 1868. He was in the business 60 years, retiring in 1953. A veteran of the Spanish-American War,[9] he was a member of United Spanish War Veterans, a life member of Elks Lodge . . . and a member of Trinity Episcopal Church, Rock Island.

---

[9] Henry was actually twenty years old at the time of the Spanish-American War, not in high school. My stories about Henry's feelings and involvement in the war are fiction.

Child: Traugott Richter (1904–1965)

Traugott Richter
(son of Henry Richter)

Traugott was fourteen when he won the spelling bee at the Iowa State Fair.

Graduate of Dartmouth College; PhD from Northwestern University; professor of English at Augustana College in Rock Island, Illinois

Married: Delores Copp
Child: One daughter

A newspaper article tells about Traugott's extensive collection of jazz recordings and music, which he started when he was a high school classmate of Bix Beiderbecke. His collection included a "rare original" of *Davenport Blues*.

Elsie (1880–1963)

Elsie Richter Oman
Keiffer

Married: Ernest Oman;

Oral History: Elsie was born in Des Moines after Marie left Traugott to live with her sister. I used her name in this story in place of Emily's sister Louise. My grandmother was very close to her half sister Elsie. When Emily was critically ill during her adult years, Elsie helped care for her and for my mom and uncle who were teenagers at that time.

Children:

Hazel (1901–1997)
Married: Delmer Aamodt
Four children

Ernest Oman (1906–1995)
Married: Laura
One daughter

In a note to my mother in 1995, Elsie's granddaughter wrote:

> I was always fascinated by the stories Grandma Keifer would tell me about her family and the big house they lived in. One of my favorite stories was about the Christmases and the big tree with candles and the firemen who came every night to light them.

Married: ? Keifer. I don't have any information about Elsie's second husband. It appears that she married him prior to 1929 and lived in California at least from that time until her death. Her son and daughter also lived in California. Her son, Ernest Oman, was at one time the mayor of Santa Paula, California.

Children of Traugott and Wilhelmina

Edward (1880–1929)

Vice president of T. Richter's Sons prior to his death at age forty-eight. Obituary refers to him as a "master furrier" and "an estimable citizen . . . a sincere and true friend."
Married: Clara Krieg
Children:
Edward (1907–1986), not married
Claus (1908–1977); married Myrtle Frantz; eight children

Frieda (1883–1961)

Married: Sam Banta
Children:
Traugott (1904–1974)
William (1906–1975)

August (1885–1980)

Married: Elizabeth
Children:
Eugene (1908–1997); three children
Allen (?)

Alma (1886–1977)

Married: William Chambers; no children

Traugott (1888–1929)

Never married; enlisted in the navy in 1907; WWI vet—sergeant in army; served on battlefields of France for eleven months

Herbert (1891–1940)

Never married

Gertrude (1895–1969)

Never married; taught school in La Salle, Illinois (perhaps business)

Children of Marie and James Bowers

Emily (1883–1961)

Born: June 17, 1883, in Denver, Colorado
Married: Horace Lawton, December 17, 1902
Died: December 25, 1961, in Davenport
Children:
Leslie (1904–1975)
Lucille Marie (1907–2007)
Mary (1908–1910)
Oral History: After the death of her mother when Emily was four years old, she and her two sisters lived with the Davis family in Rockvale, Colorado. Her half sisters and brothers returned to Davenport at that time to live with their father, Traugott, and his second wife, Wilhelmina, and their other children. Emily's father, James Bowers, remained in Denver and visited his three girls when he could. He died when Emily was eight years old. Traugott sent his oldest son, Will, to Colorado

to bring her, Lulu, and Marie back to Davenport, where he raised them with the rest of his family. At that time, Emily did not want to leave the Davis family.

She told the following story about her life in Rockvale: At Christmas the entire town gathered together at the town hall Christmas tree where presents were distributed to the children. She saw a beautiful doll under the tree, which she hoped would be for her. When the doll was given to her sister Lulu instead, she was terribly disappointed, but later an identical doll (which she had not seen on the other side of the tree) was given to her.

Traugott Richter was very good to all the children. When Emily first came to live with him, she asked if he knew her mother to which he replied, "I loved your mother." Emily said that Traugott would introduce her to his friends, saying how much she resembled her mother, Marie.

According to the stories, Wilhelmina had little involvement in raising the children, including her own. Each older child was assigned responsibility for one of the younger children. Emily was in charge of Herbert. As an adult, if any of her siblings were critical of Herbert, Emily would defend him. Emily always spoke kindly of her stepmother and visited Wilhelmina after she was married. She had great affection for all her brothers and sisters.

Emily loved school and was a good student. In seventh grade, she was awarded the Kuhnen Medal for academic achievement. Each year the school faculty chose one student to receive the award. The medal was passed on to my mother and then to me.

Emily (*top*) at age twelve, wearing the Kuhnen Medal.
Front row: Alma Richter and Louise Bowers, who also
appears to be wearing the Kuhnen Medal.

Emily wanted to be a teacher, which would have required graduating from high school and attending one year of Normal School. Traugott told her that teachers are a dime a dozen, and she had to work at the Richter store instead. I know she completed grammar school, which could have been either eighth or ninth grade, but I do not have any information about her high school education. Since she had studied Latin, perhaps she attended a few years of high school or even graduated but wasn't allowed to go on to Normal School.

At the age of nineteen, Emily married Horace Lawton. They had three children: Leslie, Lucille, and Mary, who died of diphtheria at age two. Emily was critically ill when she was thirty-eight but survived because Carl and Henry wrapped her in a fur coat and drove her to Iowa City University Hospital. Horace died in 1942, and Emily died at the age of seventy-eight on Christmas Day 1961.

The following letter was written to Emily on September 28, 1917, from Maggie Davis Jones, Rockvale, Colorado:

> My dear Emily,
> Your letter came tonight and what a pleasant surprise to hear from you girls again. How often we speak of you and wondered what had become of you all.
> Mother is away this last month visiting Mrs. Philips at the ranch. Do you remember her, my step-sister, so I will answer your letter and Mother shall write again. First of all I must tell you that we buried our father in December 1915. How he loved you girls and often wondered why he did not hear from you. When Father died we moved in with mother so we all live in the same old house that you girls did years ago. Mother is quite well. My children are grown up. Maude married seven years ago but she and her husband parted soon after. She has a boy six years old. I have had him since he was six months old. He is John M. after Father. Maude is in… [illegible] since March but expects to come back in Dec. She is working there. Ed is in college at Boulder. This is his second year.

Lottie and Roy live in Florence, she is a dressmaker, Roy is taking his second year in high school. Ella and family live on a farm 18 miles from Glenwood Springs. They are all doing well. So glad to hear of Marie and Lulu doing well and when you write to them be sure to give our fondest love to them all. Yes this war is serious. Mrs Philips second boy Clarence has been drafted on this call. It comes nearer to us when some of our own are called out. Everything is high here except potatoes, we get them now for $2.00 a hundred. Everybody is trying to raise a garden, but we did not have any. Well I think I have told you about us all so will close and do write again soon as we like to hear how you are getting along. Your boy is certainly doing well in school. I don't open mother's letters but when I saw the post mark on it I knew it was from one of you girls so I could not wait to send it to Mother before I found out how you were. Love to all.

Your Loving friend,
Maggie

Mrs. W. K. Jones[10]

---

[10] This letter from Maggie Davis Jones, one of Emily's "Colorado sisters," is the only source of information I have about the rest of the Davis family. I do not know anything about the people mentioned except what is explained in the letter. I used the name Maude for Mama Davis, Ella for the other sister, and Lottie for one of Emily's friends.

Louise/Lulu (1884–1964)

Married: Charles Dempster (1846–1929) in Omaha, Nebraska, in 1920; no children

A newspaper clipping and snapshots in my mother's scrapbook show her with Louise and Marie in Omaha in 1930. The photos also show Marie's children, John and Marie Barrett.

I changed Louise's name to Elsie, since Marie had two daughters named Louise. The Elsie in my book represents a combination of Elsie Richter and Louise Bowers.

Marie (1886–1947)

Married: John Barrett, Denver, Colorado

The 1930 census indicated that Marie was divorced, and she and her two children were living with her sister, Louise Dempster, in Omaha. In 1940 Marie was living in Omaha with her daughter, Marie.

Children:

Marie Barrett (1910–1961): Never married; Marie wrote the letter to my mother that provided information about her grandmother's life in Denver. Later in life, Marie lived in Los Angeles.

John Barrett (1913–?): Lived in Omaha with his mother in 1930 (age seventeen). No further information found.

The Lawton Family

Maurice Lawton (1818–1905)

Born: December 23, 1818, in Ireland
Married: Ellen Murry, November 12, 1856. Served as a private in the Missouri Infantry for six months during the Mexican War (1846)

Ellen Murry Lawton (1824–1916)

Born: December 20, 1824, in Ireland
Children: Mary, Margaret, Edward, and Horace (adopted)

Mary Lawton Cunningham (1852–1927)

Mary Lawton Cunningham

Married: Edward Cunningham, July 5, 1887; he died in 1892.
Oral History: It was Mary who encouraged her parents to adopt Horace, and she was primarily responsible for raising him. Horace was adopted in 1884, so Mary was thirty-two years old and single at that time. Her mother was sixty, and her

father was sixty-six. Mary was married at the age of thirty-five, and she and her husband lived in the house next door to the home where her parents lived (and where I later grew up).

Mary made the patchwork crazy quilt, which was passed on to my grandmother, then my mother, and then to me. The date, "Nov. 4th. 1884", is embroidered on one of the squares.

When Mary died, she left her property to Horace, including the Lawton home at 913 Vine Street, the house next door where she lived, and two other neighboring homes.

Mary also owned property in Glenwood Springs, Colorado, where she lived part of the time because she feared dying of tuberculosis like her sister.

My mother was very fond of her Aunt Mary, and I was named after her.

Mary Lawton Cunningham obituary: Excerpt:

> At one time she was a school teacher here (Davenport) and for many years was the cashier at McCabe's store in Rock Island. She had been both active and successful in a business way and was known to many friends as possessing a kind and charitable disposition.

Margaret Lawton Dart (1854–1878)
Married: William Dart, January 17, 1877

Edward Lawton (1859–1916)
Never married.
Occupation: Drayman (driver of a delivery wagon)
Lived at 903 Vine Street

Horace Lawton (1880–1942)

Horace Lawton
Age 4

Horace Lawton

Born: December 19, 1880, in New York City
Married: Emily Bowers on December 17, 1902
Children: See Emily
Died: January 23, 1942, in Davenport, Iowa

Oral History: Horace was brought to Davenport at the age of four on an orphan train from a Catholic orphanage (possibly the Foundling Hospital) in New York City. Twenty children were adopted by families of St. Mary's Catholic Church. I was told that he had an older sister on the train, but no one in the family knows what happened to her. It was assumed that Horace was of Irish heritage because his appearance was "black Irish," a term that refers to people from southwestern Ireland who were descendants of Spanish sailors or simply a term describing Irish people with dark hair.

Horace was a pitcher for a local semipro baseball team. He also hired out to pitch for teams in nearby small towns. One time he was pitching in a game across the Mississippi when a storm came up. He wanted to get home, but no one would row him across the river. He borrowed a boat and crossed in the storm, taking off his shoes in case he capsized and had to swim. When he reached the bank at LeClaire, Iowa, many people were lined up on the shore to see if he would make it across the river.

According to my mother, her father had an excellent singing voice, and they would sing together because she was the only other member of the family who could carry a tune. He also accompanied the two of them on a banjo or fiddle.

Horace Lawton's obituary: Excerpt:

> He was educated at St. Mary's parochial school and at St. Ambrose academy. For 23 years he had been employed at the Rock Island arsenal. Mr. Lawton was a prominent baseball pitcher in the early 1900's, playing with the Y's, the Yales and the Suburban teams.

My mother's scrapbook also has newspaper clippings and photos of Horace with some of his teams including the Pittsburg Glass Ball Club and the Marquette Sunday Morning Baseball Club. Les Lawton is named as the "mascot" for the Sunday Morning Club. One article refers to "memories of the stirring days on Mitchell's Bluff in 1912 when the novel, unique, and now historic Sunday Morning Club was in full swing." The article tells many humorous stories of the arguments that took place during the games. It also mentions Tom Walsh, "the heaviest slugger . . . and a former member of the Chicago Cubs."

Children of Horace and Emily Lawton

Emily, Horace, and Leslie

Leslie Lawton (1904–1975)

Never married

Oral History: Les loved to read and was a talented athlete. He was also a good student and studied the Latin course in high school. His mother did help him with his Latin homework. He played on basketball and baseball teams in school and later played semipro baseball. He was a left fielder. After high school, he trained as a furrier and worked at the Richter store until it was sold in 1953. Throughout his life, he lived with his mother at the 913 Vine house and was always part of our family activities. He and his Saint Bernard dog were a fixture in the neighborhood.

Leslie Lawton, Age 7

My uncle Les with Duke and me

Lucille Marie Lawton Weiss (1907–2007)

Lucille
Age 17

Born: January 21, 1907
Married: Rudolph Weiss, October 9, 1943
Died: November 2, 2007
Children:
Mary Lu Lawton Weiss (Lewis) (1944–)
Kathleen Ruth Weiss (1948–1978)
Oral History: Lucille attended Smart Intermediate School but was very unhappy that she couldn't go to J. B. Young, where her best friend went to school. However, she made life-long friends while at Smart. She wanted to drop her German class but was told by a teacher that she could never get a job if she didn't speak German. She also didn't like cooking class but loved math. She was musical just like her father and loved playing the piano throughout her life.

Horace, Emily, Lucille, and Leslie   Lawton Home at 913 Vine Street

Lucille and her 1932 Plymouth

Lucille loved to travel: she drove throughout the Midwest and as far as New York City and Yellowstone National Park as a young woman. She went on camping trips across the United States with her husband and children, and she traveled all over the world in her senior years.

At Davenport High School, Lucille was in the Commercial Course. Several years after graduating, she went to work for her Uncle Will and his sons at Ewert and Richter, where she was a secretary and bookkeeper until the day I was born. She loved her work and greatly admired her Uncle Will. She was also proud that he told her she had a good head for business just like his mother, Marie.

Lucille was devoted to her husband and family. She lovingly cared for her mother, Emily, in her later years and her handicapped daughter, Kathy, throughout her life. She kept in touch with many of her relatives with letters and cards, and she kept the family records and photos that I used for this book. She was a loving wife and mother and was involved in many activities—especially at her church. Her volunteer jobs included delivering Meals on Wheels for twenty-five years until she was ninety-two. She adored her granddaughter and lived to see her first great-grandson, who was born when she was ninety-nine years old.

Lucille and her granddaughter,
Sarah, age twenty, in 1994

Mary Lawton (1908–1910)

Mary died of diphtheria at age two.

Home of Traugott and Wilhelmina West Ninth Street

Henry C. Kahl purchased the home from the Richter estate for $15,000, possibly in 1921. A newspaper clipping states:

> The home is built of brick and stands two and one-half stories high. It was built many years ago by the late T. Richter and was occupied up until a short time ago by his widow. The property adjoins that of the new owner and has a commanding position on a high bluff overlooking the entire city.

This Ward Olson watercolor was made from the newspaper clipping.

The Richter home had been demolished by the time I was born, leaving just an empty lot that was owned by the Figge family, who lived in the house next door. (Mrs. Figge was the daughter of Henry Kahl.) In the 1950s, the Figge home was donated to the Catholic Diocese and was used as a nursing home, the Kahl Home for the Aged. An addition was built on the Richter site in the 1980s. The original home and the addition have now been renovated and turned into apartments for senior living.

View from 1025 W. Ninth in 2012, looking south toward the Mississippi River, which can be seen through the trees.

Home of Marie and Traugott Marquette Street (Marie's Castle)

A feature article, "A Feast of History" in the *Quad-Cities Times*, Feb. 9, 1979 tells about the owner's conversion of the home at 1012 Marquette Street to a restaurant. Keith Meyer had originally purchased the home in 1974 to use as a residential treatment center for adolescents. Excerpts:

It was this sweep of landscape that captured the imagination of Traugott Richter (1844-1904), the Davenport fur baron who built the home in 1879. Richter, a German immigrant, established in 1867 what today is Richter-Rhomberg furriers.

Richter sold his showplace in 1880 to lumberman Lorenzo Schricker for $12,000 plus a home Schricker owned on Farnam Street. Henry F. Petersen, a son of the founder of Petersen Harned Von Maur department store, bought the place from the Schricker family in 1888. It remained in the Petersen family until 1923.

Frank Kohrs, whose Kohrs Packing Co. is now the Oscar Mayer & Co. Davenport plant, lived in the mansion from 1925 to 1953, the year it was sold (to Gerald Eggers) for $45,000 to become a nursing home.

It remained a nursing home until Meyer bought it.

Other descriptive phrases included the following:

"Perched on a 6 1/2-acre wooded hillside overlooking the Mississippi River valley."

"Marble floored foyer and walnut stair case with its newel post goddess thrusting her torch of light."

"Double parlor with two Italian marble fireplaces, scrolled plaster ceiling and Roman columns."

"Oak paneled dining room with an ornate chandelier suspended from a sculptured rosette."

"Library with its stained glass windows, walnut woodwork and built in bookcase-secretary."

"Half dozen upstairs bedrooms."

"A narrow staircase snakes up into the tower. From this lofty roost, one has a spectacular view of the city."

The T. Richter Fur Store

Quotes from a *Daily Times* article, "Rhomberg's, Morgan Buy Richter's" June 26, 1953, concerning the sale of the store to Rhomberg's Furs of Dubuque, Iowa and Riley Morgan of Davenport, referred to Richter's as "one of the largest and oldest furriers in the Middlewest":

The Richter store is one of the oldest business firms in Davenport and was founded in 1868 by Traugott Richter when he established a small fur store at 323 West Second street. Located across from the shop was a duck pond. The store featured muffs and neckpieces from raw skins. By the time other businesses had supplanted the duck pond across the street, Richter had added millinery and men's wear to his own stock. The store was operated at the location for 30 years. When the store moved to its present location, 219-221 West Second street, the second generation including the late Carl Richter, Sr., and Henry Richter, now president, became engaged in the business. The Richter establishment is one of the largest furriers in the state and for many years manufactured its own fur pieces from skins purchased from trappers and leading furriers. It operated offices in New York and Leipzig, Germany, with customers all over the United States.

The famous Richter bear, which has become a Second street institution has been in front of the store for the past 30 years. Before acquiring the present bear, the firm had used three standing bears which were moved in and out of the store daily.

Quotes from a *Daily Times* article, "Randy, the Richter Bear Loses His Happy Home":

Randy, an Alaskan brown bear weighing about 500 pounds when he roamed the bleak northlands, was obtained by the store from the Museum of Science and Industry in Chicago in 1923. His three predecessors who guarded the entry to the Richter store since the Civil War, are believed to have been inhabitants of Scott county, although no definite information is available.

The first three bears at the Richter store were mounted on wheels and were brought in at night and wheeled out again in the mornings. It was an annual ritual at the store when the bears were given their bath, so they would present the proper appearance to passersby.

Quotes and photo from *Quad-City Times*, October 6, 1977, state that the Richter Bear

"was such an unusual sight . . . that his perch became a favorite meeting place for Quad-Citians. His status rose from stuffed critter to city landmark.

Photo of the unveiling of "a bronzed statue commemorating
the famous 'Richter Bear,' a stuffed bear that stood for half
a century in front of the old T. Richter Fur Store."

A booklet titled *Davenport: The Eastern Gateway of Iowa*
was probably written to promote business development in
Davenport. There is no copyright date on the book, but information contained in the booklet would lead me to believe that
is was written around 1910. A quote from this book, which in
all likelihood refers to the Richter Fur Store, states:

> In Davenport is located one of the great-
> est fur houses in the entire West. This house
> imports the finest and rarest furs trapped in
> the furthermost corners of the earth. Every
> year it sends its cutters to the fashion centers
> of the East, so they may keep abreast of the
> times as to style and nature of the manufac-
> tured garments that the trade demands.

The original Richter Fur Store (1868–1898) located at 323 W. Second Street. The Richter Bear is at the far left, but part of the photo is torn and missing. The second man from the left in the light vest is probably Will Richter. Traugott, also wearing a vest, is standing in the entrance next to the woman in the white dress. It is possible that the woman is Wilhelmina.

Davenport, 1888

This portion of an 1888 map of Davenport shows an area that includes Marquette, Vine, Eighth, and Ninth Streets showing Marie's Castle on Marquette, the Richter home on Ninth Street, and the Lawton home on Vine Street.

Grammar School No. 3

My grandmother and her brothers and sisters attended Grammar School No. 3, located on Sixth and Warren. Later it was named Jefferson School. In 1860 Phoebe Sudlow was the principal of both Grammar Schools No. 2 and No. 3, possibly the first woman principal of a public school in the United States. Later she became principal of the high school, the first female superintendent of schools, and the first female professor at the University of Iowa.

Factual Family Tree

Traugott Richter & Marie Schmidt
(1844–1904)   (1850–1887)
m. 1867

Nonnie	William	Carl	Louise	Marie	Henry	Elsie
(1870)	(1871–1938)	(1874–1947)	(1875–1946)	(1877)	(1878–1963)	(1880–1963)
	m. Blondina Martens	m. Jenny Kuhr	m. Henry Dunker		m. Minnie Stender	m. Ernest Oman
	William (1897–1965)	Carl (1898–1952)	Marie (1896–1959)		Traugott (1904–1965)	Hazel (1901–1997)
	Rudolph (1900–1977)	Catherine (1904–1991)	Henry (1903–1975)			Ernest (1906–1995)
		James (1908–1973)				

James Bowers & Marie Schmidt Richter
(1845–1892)   (1850–1887)
m. 1881

Emily	Louise (Lulu)	Marie
(1883–1961)	(1884–1964)	(1886–1947)
m. Horace Lawton	m. Charles Dempster	m. John Barrett

Leslie (1904–1975)	Marie (1910–1961)
Lucille (1907–2007)	John (1913–?)
Mary (1908–1910)	

Traugott Richter & Wilhelmina
(1844–1904)   (1858–1941)
m. 1880

Edward	Elfrida	August	Alma	Traugott	Herbert	Gertrude
(1880–1929)	(1883–1961)	(1885–1980)	(1886–1977)	(1888–1929)	(1891–1940)	(1895–1969)
m. Clara Krieg	m. Sam Banta	m. Elizabeth	m. William Chambers			

Edward (1907–1986)	Traugott (1904–1974)	Eugene (1908–1997)
Claus (1908–1977)	William (1906–1975)	Allen (?)

Acknowledgments

There are many people I would like to thank for their input and support. A special thanks to my husband and daughter, who read my earliest drafts and gave advice that helped make the story more comprehensible. I love you and appreciate your support. David Michaels motivated me by example to start this project that had been incubating in my mind for years. Thanks to my friends, Betty who was my first editor and Pat who provided advice on publishing. Jim Schebler from the Davenport School Museum helped me with researching the educational system in Davenport and found references to various members of the Richter family. The staff in the Genealogy and History Department of the Davenport Public Library helped me locate newspaper articles about family members. Several of my friends from Davenport did everything from trekking around Davenport with me when I was starting my research to encouraging me through every step of the process. Tucson friends helped with research, read early versions, and offered both advice and suggestions, which were greatly appreciated. I would also like to thank everyone who politely listened to me talk about this project and those who read the original printed version of the story and then encouraged me to publish it. Finally, thanks to Sarah, Chris, Nick, and Kayla—they are the reason I wrote this book. More than any other motivation, I wanted to share with them the stories about their ancestors and some of the values that are important to me, values passed on by my parents. I also wanted to express the love that parents feel for their children and grandchildren—the love I have for each of them.

With sincere appreciation,
Mary Lewis

About the Author

Mary Lewis is a native of Davenport, Iowa, where three previous generations of her family lived. She is a graduate of Iowa State University and Clarke College in Dubuque, Iowa. She taught elementary school primarily in River Forest, Illinois, for twenty-seven years. She and her husband, Terry, retired to Tucson, Arizona. They have one daughter and three grandchildren. Her motivation in writing this book was to share with her grandchildren stories she heard about her grandmother and great-grandmother and to exemplify a family's love for one another. She hopes her book will motivate others to search for and preserve family history and to share personal stories with their children and grandchildren.

CPSIA information can be obtained
at www.ICGtesting.com
Printed in the USA
LVHW01s0017290518
578821LV00003B/165/P